NORTHWEST NURSE

Nurse Holly Doran wasn't entirely sure that psychiatrist Dr. Brian Merdahl was for her. A temporary assignment, far away in Oregon, seemed to be the answer. If she was away from Brian for three months, she would know if she really loved him . . . Ocean Breeze, Oregon, was full of surprises for Holly — she hadn't expected to like small-town life so much and she had never dreamed that the doctor she was to work with would be as young and as attractive as Dr. Key Catrell!

ARLENE FITZGERALD

NORTHWEST NURSE

Complete and Unabridged

LINFORD
Leicester

First published in the
United States of America

First Linford Edition
published August 1993

British Library CIP Data

Fitzgerald, Arlene
    Northwest nurse.—Large print ed.—
Linford romance library
I. Title II. Series
813.54 [F]

ISBN 0–7089–7453–8

Published by
F. A. Thorpe (Publishing) Ltd.
Anstey, Leicestershire

Set by Words & Graphics Ltd.
Anstey, Leicestershire
Printed and bound in Great Britain by
T. J. Press (Padstow) Ltd., Padstow, Cornwall

This book is printed on acid-free paper

1

THE road swooped above the vast Pacific, following the flounced contours of the Coast Range. Then, just as suddenly, it dipped down to a broad harbor, formed by the wide mouth of a river that curved back from the sea, deceivingly silent, as smooth and shiny as satin ribbon, between high, green mountains.

To the west, toward the setting sun, the rocky ocean cliffs ended abruptly, near the river's mouth, dwindling into a long, driftwood-banked stretch of beach. Long, gray, ramshackle buildings crouched in the drifted sand, all but obscured by a mat of salt loving vine. A pier jutted out from them, rickety, its missing planks letting bright splotches of light through to illuminate the oily, dark water beneath it.

A heap of scrap smoldered at the

head of the pier. A sign on the most substantial of the decrepit buildings read, "Jinx Jones, Wrecking Yard."

The vista on the far side of the harbor seemed more promising. A cluster of buildings, picturesque in the slanting rays of light, nestled on a point of land below a jutting headland. High on the cape, beyond the salt-washed little community, the paned windows of a gabled mansion glittered seaward in the evening sun.

Holly Doran, R.N., pressed her face to the bus window, a wave of excitement sweeping through her, culminating in the sparkling depths of her blue eyes. Ocean Breeze. The name suited the small place well. The very atmosphere smacked of sea and salt and sand, mingled with the cloyingly sweet perfume of wild azaleas and Oregon broom. Redwood grew back from the sea, in the moist, river valley, sheltering a veritable jungle of lesser greenery.

The bus crossed a long, narrow drawbridge, set on concrete pillars above the sulky, green water. Holly glimpsed a sawmill upstream, its wigwam burners belching gusts of blue-gray smoke, its yards stacked with neat piles of russet-colored lumber. Lenhart and Sons. The name was splashed across the endless roof of a drying kiln, in ten-foot high letters.

The bus pulled into town, and came to a gasping halt before a dowdy cafe. "This is it, Miss," the driver hooked a steady hand through Holly's elbow, and helped her down the high steps, taking her bags inside the cafe.

Holly stood on the sidewalk, as the bus drove away, her blue eyes curious. She had written to the Ocean Breeze Chamber of Commerce, before she left San Francisco, not wanting to arrive in a strange town totally unprepared. Mill and resort town, the brochure had said.

She smiled to herself, as she waited, thinking that Ocean Breeze was certainly a world removed from the resort towns she was accustomed to — Santa Cruz, with its spacious, palm lined streets. Or Monterey ... But, then, she hadn't come to Ocean Breeze on a pleasure trip, she reminded herself, taking Dr. Key Catrell's letter from her purse. It read:

Thank you for your prompt response to my plea for help. As you may have assumed, after reading my ad in the Examiner, I am in dire need of a good R.N. A full time, medical assistant might describe my needs more accurately ... I will look forward to an interview with you, soon. If you will wire me, collect, of your arrival time, I will arrange to meet you.

A tingling of excitment danced through her at the prospect of meeting the man who had penned those decisive words. She tucked the letter into her purse, her eyes seeking the comforting lines of a hospital, set against the shadowy, coastal greenery. There was no such reassuring edifice of the type Holly was accustomed to. Only the weathered houses, most of them surprisingly, and anciently Victorian, beyond the row of salt encrusted business buildings.

Dr. Catrell hadn't mentioned a hospital in his letter. But surely the small town had a medical plant of some sort. She brushed the thought aside, glancing at the round face of the nurse's watch, nestled beneath the spotless cuff of the ascot shirt she had chosen to wear with her tweed travel suit. A vague feeling, that she recognized as fear, trembled through her, now that she was here, in the strange little town. She went inside the cafe, where her luggage was stacked — enough uniforms and casual clothes, with a daring, red cocktail dress tucked in for good measure — to keep her decent for a month or two, or however long she decided to stay in Ocean Breeze. If she decided to stay at all, after she had met Dr. Key Catrell . . .

"Coffee while you wait?" The waitress' voice broke through her thoughts. "It's on the house, for bus passengers."

Holly said, "Yes, please," slipping onto one of the high stools to sip the hot brew, wondering whether Dr. Catrell would prove to be young, or elderly, trying to formulate a picture of him in her mind.

Dr. Key Catrell. The name gave her no hint of what she might expect. It *could* very well belong to a dedicated old family practitioner, as Brian had chosen to believe. She had shown the letter to Dr. Brian Merdahl, before she left San Francisco. "No young doctor would be fool enough to stick himself off up there in the Oregon boondocks, when there are countless city pigeons to be plucked," the handsome psychiatrist had stated. "I say your man's an oldster. Otherwise, I might not encourage your little excursion into the wilderness in search of your true self. Of course, I'll expect you to see some men," he had added, a relenting smile angling across his lean face. "Just a single word of caution, sweetheart. Don't see too much of any one man. That sort of thing can become a habit."

Brian was right on that score, Holly thought. *He* had certainly become a habit with her. Enough of a habit for her to accept his ring, when he asked her to marry him. Except that her engagement to Dr. Brian Merdahl had proved to be a disappointment. Somewhere along the way, the sweetness and light had gone out of their romance. For her, at any rate . . . She tacked on the thought, remembering why she was here in this strange, moldering little ocean community.

"In search of your true self . . . " Brian's words still rang in her ears. Impersonal words, she thought, as though she were one of his disturbed psychiatry patients. Someone like Felicia Onstott, for instance. She had never cared for the blond, cat-like society girl, who consumed one of Dr. Brian Merdahl's thirty dollar hours each week, and who was in the habit of calling him between appointments, to discuss, with startling frankness, her love life, or whatever else happened to occupy her darting mind at the moment.

Holly had known, when she gave up her job at Mercy Hospital, to go to work in Brian's penthouse office, at the top of the Schyler Building, that she would come in for her share of analysis. Brian, as one of San Francisco's leading young psychiatrists, had definite ideas about the patterns the lives of his acquaintances, as well as his patients, should follow.

"On the house," he had modified his verbal insights into her character. He seemed to assume that, because she had accepted a glittering, two carat diamond from him — a diamond tucked safely away in her parents' safety deposit box at the First Federal Bank, for the duration of her 'vacation' — that it became his privilege to examine her id and ego at will. Being engaged to a man like Brian had its difficulties, Holly thought. His outlook and ideas were quite a thing apart from those of other, more ordinary men.

She was down to the dregs in her coffee cup, when the cafe door flew open, and a young man breezed in, bringing with him a thrust of cool, salt laden air. He was tall, with hair as dark as her own, crisp, whereas hers was silky. Faded denim trousers, topped by a white shirt, emphasized the clean length of his legs. The shirt gaped open below his Adam's apple, revealing a dense patch of hair. Spotless cuffs turned back on brown, sinewy arms, accented his rugged virility.

"Miss Doran?" Eyes the same restless shade as a stormy sea caught and held her own.

"Yes, I'm Miss Doran," she told him, thinking that Dr. Catrell hadn't come to meet her, after all, that he had sent this dark haired, denim clad man in his stead. Disappointment tugged at the corners of her mind, making inroads on her composure. She had hoped to view the doctor away from his working environment. It would have been easier, then, to evaluate his character as a man, apart from the sterile, iodoform scented atmosphere of a medical office. Since she would be working closely with him, if she accepted the job he offered, it seemed important to her to know what kind of a person he might be, aside from his capacities as an M.D.

"I'm sorry I'm late," the casually attired man told her. "It wasn't intentional, I assure you." He reached for her bags, stacked near the cafe door.

"If you'll explain that to the doctor for me," Holly smiled, thinking that his voice was surprisingly rich and well modulated for a deck hand's. For obviously, the man worked around the dock she had seen jutting into the harbor. He *had* to be a seaman, with a tan like that. "Promptness is a necessary virtue in a nurse," she added.

"I know," he grinned, flecks of amusement sparkling in the depths of his gray eyes. "I should have introduced myself, Miss Doran. Key Catrell M.D." He set aside one of the bags, and shot out a brown hand. She noticed, for the first time, the spatulate fingers, the half moons showing on closely clipped, oval nails, the sprinkling of dark hair along the tan arms, gleaming crisply clean below the spotless, white shirt sleeves.

"I . . . I expected someone older," she managed, her hand tingling from his powerful clasp, sensing an intangible force in this towering, dark-haired man, as he released her limp fingers, to retrieve the bag and push open the cafe door.

She went with him, to a battered pickup truck, wondering what Brian would say, if he could see this doctor who needed a nurse so desperately he had advertised far afield to find one. Brian had wanted to drive her to Ocean Breeze; to make an interlude of the trip for both of them. She had been *afraid* to let him do that. She hadn't wanted to be alone with him, all of those long, lonely hours that it would have taken to traverse the narrow, coastal highway northward. His persistent lovemaking, that had become frighteningly demanding of late, was partially responsible for her presence in Ocean Breeze. She needed time away from the man she was engaged to marry, to evaluate her true feelings for him. A woman shouldn't feel fear, when the man she loved wanted to make love to her. To that extent, she agreed with Brian's 'on the house' analysis of her personality complexes. Lately, she had felt like a moth pinned beneath the searching lens of a microscope, whenever he turned his smoldering, dark eyes on her.

She smiled, feeling glad that he *hadn't* come, as she climbed into the vintage truck beside Dr. Key Catrell.

2

THEY drove north, through town past curio shops, their windows decorated with fishnet and driftwood, displaying an assortment of dried sea life and priceless items fashioned from driftwood burls and myrtlewood; past two new motels, neon-lighted, flashing vacancy signs, and a big new restaurant that shamed the bus-stop cafe.

Canvas banners, with orange flowers painted on them, plopped against the breeze, suspended between street lamps. "Our Azalea Festival is coming up in a couple of weeks," Dr. Catrell explained. "This place will be hopping, then. Flowers everywhere. And pretty girls. It opens our tourist season. You'd be surprised at the number of visitors it draws."

"It sounds fascinating," Holly commented, trying to imagine the dead little town alive with people.

"I'm glad you came, Miss Doran," Dr. Catrell said. "You have to like us." It was a statement as decisive as the letter folded inside of her tightly clutched purse. "We have everything to offer the city weary, if you happen to fall into that well-worn category. Surf. Sand. Sun. Everything but adequate medical facilities. I'm trying to do something about that. You're the only R.N. who answered my ad. That makes you important."

"I didn't see a hospital," Holly said, thinking that she should feel flattered. Instead, she felt queasy inside, with a gnawing little fear that she refused to recognize. Resort town or not, Ocean Breeze was remote. More isolated than she had imagined, when she impulsively answered Dr. Catrell's ad in the Examiner. And the strange, handsome M.D. beside her was unlike any doctor she had ever known, in his faded denims and utility truck.

Darkness surrounded them, falling

suddenly, an eerie, black curtain, punctuated by the vague shapes of wind-gnarled spruce. Only the sea, visible beyond the stark, windswept headland, retained traces of light, glimmering faintly along the crests of great, surging waves.

"There is none," his rich voice sounded unperturbed. "Unless you want to count my office set-up. It's hardly a match for your big city medical plants. But it serves the purpose, for the time being."

"I don't understand, Doctor," Holly said, in a soft, puzzled voice. "How can you carry on a practice here, with no hospital for your surgical patients? Your O.B.'s?"

"I'm on the staff at Seal Beach General. It's really not so far down there," he added, sensing what her next question would be. "An hour's drive, unless there happens to be fog."

The bus had passed through Seal Beach, what seemed to Holly like hours ago, so widely separated were the small,

15

coastal communities. Not one of the seaside hamlets had appeared to have more than five hundred inhabitants, including Ocean Breeze. "How can such a small place support an M.D.?" she wondered.

"I'm under contract to Lenhart and Sons to look after their employees," Dr. Catrell explained. "Beyond that, you'd be surprised at the number of people scattered along these windy, coastal stretches. Fifteen hundred, maybe two thousand in this area alone. And the tourist trade is coming into its own. Everyone is sprucing up for the onslaught, turning out myrtlewood art work, and building new motels. I've invested in some badly needed office equipment, and I'm importing an R.N. My preparations aren't the kind that show."

He paused, and she sensed that he was smiling at her through the darkness. "Correction, Miss Doran," he said, his vibrant voice impulsive. "*You* definitely will be a visible asset, if you decide to stay on here as my nurse-assistant. A very striking and valuable asset, if I may say so."

An almost boyish shyness tinged his husky voice, striking at her heart with sudden appeal, vanishing any reservations she may have had. She was going to like this man, she thought, tossing caution to the winds, feeling a growing eagerness to learn more about his practice, in this vagrant section of country that seemed a world apart from anything she had ever known.

Lights appeared around a crook in the road, a mile beyond the Lenhart mansion, hovering so near the brink of the headland that they seemed almost to be suspended above the crashing sea. The uniform buildings of a motel crouched in the dense shadow of an immense, wind-crooked spruce. A sign, neonlighted, flashed bravely in the wind. 'Headland Motel', it said. And below it, in contrasting letters, 'Cafe'.

It wasn't until Dr. Catrell had pulled the pickup to a stop before one of the grayed units that Holly saw the smaller sign, a modest, redwood shingle, with letters gouged into it and outlined in white paint. It was neat and attractive, she had to admit, for all of its simplicity. Key Catrell, it read, M.D.

"This is it." He got out, and came around to open the truck's creaking door for her.

She stepped out into the sea-misted air, aware of the strong, patient pounding of the surf, sounding frighteningly near. There was no sign of any other person; no life other than that of the pushing waves below the headland.

"I . . . How far are we from town?" she asked, stifling a feeling of panic.

"This is still town," he told her, a grin lifting the corners of his square mouth. "The city limits sign is just up the road. Whoever plotted this city had great expectations. Who knows? With the population explosion, they might come true."

"I meant . . . "

"I know," he interrupted her, his

18

face growing serious, in the sketchy light from the sign. "It's five minutes to the heart of Ocean Breeze. The first time over any strange road always seems twice as far as it really is. I've made it in three, behind the wheel of the ambulance. The Lenharts have one at the mill," he added, seeing the question in her blue eyes. "It comes in handy, when an emergency arises, and I'm pressed to get a patient to Seal Beach in a hurry. But you'll discover these things for yourself . . . "

She sensed that he had been going to add, 'if you stay,' and had decided against it. He hooked a hand through her elbow, and guided her toward the end unit of the motel; the one bearing his modest shingle beside its door. He was turning the knob, when the door to a unit farther down the row burst open, and a girl came running toward them, her long hair carried on the wind like a banner.

"Key! Thank goodness you're back!" She hurried up to them, clutching a flowered wrapper across full breasts. "There's been an accident at the mill. One of the men fell into the edger saw. He was pushed, actually . . . "

"Are they bringing him here?" His rich voice cut across hers.

The girl — woman, really, Holly revised the thought, taking note of the voluptuous curves, visible beneath the flimsy wrapper, and the knowing face, wondering what her relationship might be to Dr. Catrell — shook her head, the silken lengths of hair whipping to veil her green eyes. "They said for you to come. I told them you'd . . . "

Dr. Catrell pushed open the door to his office, not waiting to hear the rest. Holly followed him, forgetting the wild-haired woman, her alert nurse's mind instantly tabulating the supplies they would need to care for a severe, bleeding wound.

"Everything we'll need is here." He guessed her thoughts, gesturing with a scarred, black bag.

Seconds later, they were whipping

through the darkness toward the mill she had seen earlier, cutting off of the main road, just below the headland, to follow a well used, graveled thoroughfare. The sweep of light from the truck's headlamps sliced the night blackness, illuminating moist, overhanging greenery, gilding the sinewy brown form of a deer.

The swing shift had shut down the mill by the time they arrived. A group of men clustered around the ambulance that had been backed up to the entrance of the main building, their faces stiffly somber in the orange glow cast by the wigwam burner. Holly detected a look of surprise in the eyes of several of them, as they drew back in a body to let her and Dr. Catrell pass.

"We'll need that stretcher," he snapped, not slowing his long-legged stride.

Two men separated themselves from the group, to slide it from the long red and white vehicle. "We'd have brought Pete to you, Doc," one of

21

them said. "But Les won't let us near him. Said he'd kill anybody who tried to move him. He's in there now, with Pete."

"Those head shrinkers he went to didn't seem to help much," someone else said. "Karl ain't going to like him shutting the mill down this way, especially when he finds out why."

Holly remembered what the woman at the motel had said about the wounded man having been pushed into the edger saw. If the man who had done it had been under psychiatric treatment . . . A sudden horror constricted her throat, as she followed Dr. Catrell inside of the immense, echoing building. She clamped the feeling of panic with firm nurse's discipline, aware of the two men close behind her, their footsteps ringing hollowly on the raised catwalk that ringed the great pits of mammoth machinery. Everything about the mill, designed to turn the monstrous redwood timbers into usable products, was oversized. The building itself seemed miles long, lighted by fluorescent tubes set on beams, below a peaked roof.

Dr. Catrell ran along the narrow walk, his manner familiar, as though he had come into the mill under these same circumstances many times before. Holly hurried her own steps, to keep pace with him, her blue eyes searching the shadows for some sign of the injured man. There was no time to dwell on the sudden fright that had squeezed around her throat at the thought of any man deliberately forcing another into the hungry, whirring blades of the savage-looking saws. It was unbelievable, even in a place so remote as Ocean Breeze.

Halfway down the length of the long shed, a dark form came into view, kneeling over a prone figure. There was an eerie quality about the scene; a macabre unreality that increased as Holly drew near enough to see the kneeling man. He was immense, his great shoulders forming a shielding bulwark above the wounded man. No wonder the men outside had hesitated to approach him!

"What's happened here, Les?" Dr. Catrell vaulted from the catwalk, onto the saw platform, where the wounded man lay, his body coordinating in one fluid, springing movement.

"Pete's got a bad cut." The man was young, with the classic features of an Adonis, so striking that Holly's breath caught in her throat, as he turned toward her. Blue-white eyes burned in a bronzed face.

She lowered her own eyes, thinking that the man could very well be a mental case, with eyes like that, seeing, in the same instant, the pool of arterial blood coagulated around the deep gash in the wounded man's leg. Already, Dr. Catrell's hands had moved in to unfasten the tourniquet someone had cinched into the thick, fleshy thigh above the oozing slash.

"I did what I could for him," the

blond man said, his strange eyes still on Holly's face. "This is no place for a girl," he added, the tone of his voice changing subtly, taking on warmth and appeal.

"Miss Doran is a nurse, Les," Dr. Catrell said, his words clipped. His broad fingers probed the flesh around the wound, determining the extent of the damage.

Holly smoothed her snug, tweed skirt along trim thighs, and squatted to slide under the catwalk railing. The blond man sprang forward at once, reaching out a sinewy arm to help her. "I'm Les Lenhart," he said.

One of the lumber people, Holly thought, seeing that he wasn't actually so immense as he had seemed at first glance. He wasn't a great deal taller than Dr. Catrell. It was the muscles, clearly visible across the broad field of his chest and back, rippling beneath the thin stuff of a knit shirt, that made him seem gigantic. Muscles flexed and corded along his bare arms, as he lifted her almost bodily, from the catwalk, and deposited her beside the patient, his blue-white eyes never leaving her face.

She knelt at once beside Dr. Catrell, reaching to take the patient's pulse, her alert eyes determining the extent of shock. Prostration. Pallor. Perspiration. She tabulated the symptoms, her darting hand dipping into the black bag for the stimulant Dr. Catrell ordered.

"The bone isn't involved, thank God." Dr. Catrell placed a pressure bandage over the gaping wound, relief showing in every line of his rugged face. "We'll get him to Seal Beach and do an inosculation." He glanced at Les Lenhart. "Call General for us, Les, and tell them to set up in surgery."

"I've already taken care of that." A bright-eyed little man, as frail as Les Lenhart was robust, came toward them along the catwalk, his small feet clad in rubber-soled sneakers, a white skipper's cap perched jauntily on one side of his gray head. "How bad is he, Key?"

"His leg is gashed, Captain. He's in shock," Dr. Catrell added tersely, helping the two men with the stretcher, cautioning them, in low tones, as they lifted the patient's prostrate body.

"Did you have to come in here and start trouble?" The small man's penetrating gaze darted to Les Lenhart's handsome face.

"He started it, Dad. Pete jumped me," Les said.

It seemed unbelievable that the dapper little man, so slight as to be almost feminine, could have fathered the big, blond man who stood over him, bronzed, god-like, turning his fiery gaze on the two mill workers who handled the stretcher.

"That's right, Captain," one of the stretcher bearers responded. "Pete jumped Les all right." The man's seamed face remained expressionless.

"They wanted to take Pete to Doc's first thing," Les said. "I knew he'd bleed to death before they got there.

I chased them out and gave him first aid. Put on a tourniquet." For all of his muscled masculinity, he reminded Holly of a little boy, cowering before authority, trying to justify himself.

"You been fooling around Pete Howe's daughter again, Les?" The little man ignored his son's explanation. "Is that what's behind this?"

"I guess a guy can date who he wants, so long as she's willing."

"Pete warned you, Les. And I'm warning you, now. Stay away from Margaret Howe."

Dr. Catrell helped the two men lift the stretcher onto the catwalk, and turned to assist Holly over the low railing with hands that gripped her small waist like hands of steel. They hurried off, leaving father and son alone on the empty catwalk, still arguing.

"Easy, now, Pete," Dr. Catrell said softly, crawling into the back of the ambulance, indicating that Holly should ride in front with the driver — one of the men who had helped carry Pete Howe from the mill. His name, he told Holly, as she climbed in beside him, was Joe Green.

3

THEY sped along the river, into the heart of town, and across the narrow drawbridge. Down the coast, fifty miles as the crow flies — farther, by car, or ambulance — to a hospital, where doctors and nurses and bright lights waited. If only it weren't so far, Holly couldn't help thinking, hearing the patient's labored breathing behind her, knowing that his condition was growing worse with every second that passed. He had lost far too much blood . . .

"Somebody should trim Les Lenhart down to size," Joe Green said, unexpectedly, shattering the tense silence that had fallen over them. "Captain's not big enough. And Karl won't."

"Karl has his hands full running the mill for Captain, without worrying about Les," Dr. Catrell said.

"Just the same, Les has no business chasing after Margaret. Just because she got chose to be Ocean Breeze's Azalea Queen this year, Les thinks that makes the girl public property. I don't blame Pete for jumping him."

"The Azalea Queen and her court have a chaperone," Dr. Catrell said, his husky voice diplomatic.

"She can't be with the girls night and day," Joe said. "Pete being a widower, and on the swing shift at the mill, that leaves Margaret free to do as she pleases most nights. Pete's been complaining lately that Les has been seen driving past their place in that red sports job of his, every chance he gets. You'd think he could find a woman his own age, without having to chase after teenage girls."

"We have a patient here, Joe," Dr. Cantrell said, his voice firm. "This kind of talk isn't doing him any good."

A little banner of fear trailed through Holly, at the sound of Pete Howe's stentorian breathing. If only it weren't so far, she found herself thinking, again.

★ ★ ★

It took them an hour to reach the modern, thirty bed hospital in Seal Beach. Joe Green pulled the ambulance up to the emergency entrance. White coated orderlies appeared almost simultaneously to wheel the patient through the gaping doors. Dr. Catrell jumped out and followed, staying close beside the litter, his big hand testing Pete Howe's responses, even as he strode along.

Holly, not quite certain what might be expected of her, under the circumstances — she was, after all, only a visitor to the area, and they would have a full operating team assembled, by now — slid out of the ambulance, and went inside. Dr. Catrell had disappeared, with the orderlies and patient.

The intercom on the emergency room desk crackled, and a woman's voice barked an icy order. "Send Dr. Catrell's nurse up," it said. "Tell her to be ready to assist him in surgery."

"But . . . " The protest died in Holly's throat. A doctor was counting on her, to use the knowledge and skills she had spent four dedicated years acquiring, and she must be ready. It made no difference that she hadn't yet voiced a decision about whether or not she would stay in Ocean Breeze as his nurse assistant.

"Nurse's scrub is the first door to the right of the elevator," the plump, matronly nurse on duty told her. "Your things will be all right in the lounge. Just pick a locker . . . "

Not bothering with the elevator, Holly ran up the stairs, found the proper door, and darted inside. The nurse's lounge and adjoining scrubroom were small, but both rooms were spotless and efficient. She stripped down, stowing the ascot shirt and tweed suit in an empty locker, and disappeared into the scrub room, clad only in panties and bra to scour lavishly with a stiff brush and germicidal solution. A licensed, practical nurse, pert in a rustling uniform, wearing her pin proudly, was ready with a surgical cap and gown when she finished.

"Lucky Dr. Catrell brought you with him, tonight," the middle-aged L.P.N. said. "We couldn't reach our surgical nurse. Either she's not at home, or her telephone is out of order."

Holly went to the door that opened into a green-tiled operating theater, and glanced through the glass panel. Pete Howe was on the table, an intravenous stand feeding pale, whitish-yellow liquid into his basilic vein. Dextran, Holly thought, automatically, until they could type and cross-match, for a transfusion of whole blood.

The operating team worked quietly, the anesthetist at the head of the table, his keen eyes bright above the edge of his breathing mask, intent on gauges and dials, as he administered a high concentration of oxygen, to combat shock. A second nurse, green-gowned, masked, prepared instrument trays. Holly moved to assist her, feeling in her element, a part of the drama that was taking place in the shining, green-tiled room.

She hadn't realized before how much she missed the sterile clank of gleaming instruments being hastily assembled for an emergency, with a smooth efficiency that left no room for hesitancy, awkwardness, or error.

Dr. Catrell entered the room, transformed by the wrinkled scrub suit and trousers, his crisp hair captured beneath the close-fitting surgical cap, his square, decisive mouth covered by the gauze breathing mask. Holly would have known him, she thought, for all of his changed appearance, by the steady, gray eyes above the mask, not missing a single detail of the O.R. preparation. Another doctor, not quite so tall as Dr. Catrell, or so handsome, Holly guessed, noticing the beginnings of a stomach protruding beneath the scrub clothes, followed him. Countless fine lines sprayed around the older doctor's faded eyes. He took his place across the table from Dr. Catrell, working brown milled surgical gloves onto hands that were a paradox, with thick, pudgy palms, and fine, slim fingers.

"Dr. Spencer," Dr. Catrell told Holly, his husky voice calm. "He assists with all of my tough ones."

"We exchange favors." The faded eyes smiled benevolently on her, for a brief second, before he turned his attention to their patient. "Key tells me you're his new nurse. It's time he found someone to help him out up there on the headland." His slow, gruff voice denied the quick movements of his hands, as he stooped to examine Pete Howe's leg.

The saw had sliced through the millworker's solid flesh, striking his leg at an angle, biting within a hair's breadth of the femur, the jagged teeth shredding tissue unmercifully.

"He's lucky," Dr. Spencer muttered

through his mask. "You might have had trouble getting this leg to mend properly, if that saw had gone through the femur."

"I've injected one percent procaine around the injury, the anesthetist reported. "The patient has also been given intravenous piminodine anesthesia."

Dr. Catrell nodded, and, without preamble, began segregating severed fibers with the gleaming instrument Holly slapped against his waiting palm, his keen, surgeon's fingers following the flow of her own gloved hand in a continuous motion, weaving them together in that inexplicable manner that fuses the members of an operating team into a working whole. Their hands intermeshed over the wound, gracefully, expertly, each brown glove flashing in its turn, performing the miracle that must be performed if Pete Howe was to live to have the full use of his leg again. Holly anticipated the need for retractors, even before Dr. Catrell could indicate, with a husky murmur, and a subtle nod, that one was needed.

He located the parted ends of the femoral artery, and reached for long, slender, coarctation clamps. With lightning swiftness, he placed them over the artery ends, freeing Miss Lucas to go into circulation. Hot, saline soaked towels were needed — and ready, in a surprisingly short time — to be placed on the skin edges to keep them moist and pliant, and to protect them while the two doctors worked in the depths of the wound, drawing the ragged ends of severed vessels and nerves from the mangled flesh, separating them from the stringy, white bits of aponeurotic covering — that strong, fibrous sheath which encases vessels and nerves securely, in that portion of the thigh known as Hunter's canal.

"B.P.R. 120 over 70." The anesthetist's routine report of vital O.R. statistics broke the silence that had fallen between them, as they concentrated all of their medical skill and energy in

38

the tips of clever fingers that teased the patch of raw flesh revealed by the split in the green, surgical sheet, back to some semblance of normalcy.

"It's come up somewhat," Dr. Catrell's voice echoed satisfaction. He reached for scissors, to trim the jagged artery ends. Holly slapped the blunt-nosed instrument into his palm, and reached to prepare needle holders, and fine, untwisted lengths of parafine treated silk, for the retraction sutures.

His hand darted out, in the same instant, for the waiting silk. She placed the needle holder in his palm, heaving a silent little sigh of gratitude for two adept hands, and a well trained mind to guide them. She realized, in the part of her mind that stood off from the urgent activity around the table, that she wanted to make a good impression on the tall, gray-eyed doctor beside her. It was important to her that her work be deft and keen, and spontaneous enough to totally satisfy him. She *wanted* to stay and work with him, in Ocean Breeze, that remote part of her mind told her. And she would — if he wanted her, after having witnessed her flying hands in action. There was no reason why he shouldn't . . .

The corners of her mind grasped the thought, holding it, bolstering her confidence in herself, as a top flight R.N., capable of coping with any medical emergency. Confidence, she knew, was an integral part of any successful nurse's makeup. It was a quality acquired gradually, during the long, hard process of becoming a qualified, graduate nurse. The nurse who failed to build confidence in herself and her abilities, could be a detriment, in an emergency. One uncertain slip of the hand, a single moment of hesitancy, could spell the difference between life and death . . .

The stay sutures were in ready to be grasped by her steady, gloved hands, and drawn taut, pyramiding the red artery walls so that the open ends peaked into tiny triangles that could be fitted together with some measure of precision, and inosculated to permit blood to be forced through the length of Pete Howe's thick leg once more. It was a sturdy leg, one that needed perfect circulation to keep it well and strong and able.

Holly watched, as Dr. Catrell began the everting intimal-to-intimal approximation of the artery ends. His hand raised for the intricate bit of arterial work. Holly's own certain grip tightened on the stay sutures, applying the necessary tension. Or what she had determined to be the proper tension . . . For in that next, horrifying second, one of the retraction sutures unexpectedly slashed through the artery layers, pulling free, allowing the neat little pyramid to collapse around the careful, dark suture Dr. Catrell was in the process of applying.

"Damn it, nurse! Is that the best you can do?" His voice, its huskiness keened to razor sharpness, lashed out at her.

Hot tears burned unexpectedly behind her eyelids. Had the long, idle months in Brian's office dulled her skill? A sick feeling spiraled through her. "Sorry, doctor," she murmured, swallowing, forcing herself to carry on, in spite of the tears that threatened to spill over. There was nothing else to say. They would have to start over; take out the remaining stays, and trim away the little tattered shred of vessel torn free by the slashing suture.

The hard core of confidence she had been so proud of only seconds before began to ooze away inside of her. Maybe it had been misplaced, under the circumstances. It had been months since she had done active surgical duty. She reached for the shiny, curved scissors, her hand surprisingly sure and steady, in spite of everything, and slapped them against his reaching palm.

The loud, raspy breathing of the patient rattled against her eardrums, almost accusingly, as though Pete Howe somehow knew that she had failed. Stay sutures had torn free before — some patients had weaker tissues than others. And she had been chastised before, by an intent M.D. There wasn't a nurse living who hadn't been, no matter how good she might be, or how confident. But this time was different. She had wanted to impress Dr. Catrell.

She reached in again, for the new sutures Dr. Catrell had applied with amazing facility, avoiding his storm-colored eyes, keeping her own gaze intent on the field of operation. She drew them taut, biting a corner of her lip, beneath her gauze breathing mask, holding her breath, as she pyramided the shining vessel.

This time, they held.

Dr. Catrell used a continuous, over and over suture, placing the neat, dark stitches in a pattern that would have done justice to any woman's fancy work. His tanned arms looked even darker beneath the dazzling brilliance of the overhead lights; his hands, in the sheath-fitting rubber gloves, seeming smaller than they had seemed before, their spatulate tips as agile as any surgeon's hands she had ever watched in action. And she had witnessed some of the best, at Mercy.

Brief moments later, the sutures were in; the insoculation finished. Now for the removal of the retraction sutures . . . Holly watched, as Dr. Catrell's gloved hands brought them free, with an adroit movement. The coarctation clamps next. Dr. Spencer attended to that detail. And they all held their breath — she could *feel* Dr. Catrell's intensity, as he bent over the operative field, studying the repair, as blood surged suddenly through the femoral, his keen, gray eyes alert for the merest bit of red beading that would mean the stitches hadn't held.

She concentrated on the pulsating artery. It had to be snug: to hold . . .

The patient was enduring well, thanks to the life giving flow being fed into his basilic vein. But the sooner they finished, the better. And they had already had one delay. She was acutely aware of the tall, green swathed doctor beside her, lifting his bent shoulders, emitting a sigh of satisfaction through the breathing mask.

"It'll do," he said.

They were safe, then. She let out her breath slowly, relief flooding through her.

"Fine work, Key." Dr. Spencer's gruff voice vibrated through the room. "He'll have no trouble with the circulation in this leg, now."

Dr. Catrell seemed not to have heard the older doctor, as he began repair of the long, saphenous nerve, concentrating all of his attention on that tedious bit of surgery. Seconds later, they were ready to close, knowing that within a matter of days, the artery and nerve ends would seal themselves naturally, and be as good as new — thanks to Dr. Catrell's skill, Holly couldn't help thinking.

A final report on respiration, pulse and

blood pressure, from the anesthetist, and they could all straighten tired shoulder muscles, and relax.

"That does it," Dr. Catrell said, slipping off his breathing mask, letting it dangle. "Pete should be up and around in a few days."

Holly busied herself in the small, sparkling room, helping Miss Lucas with the instruments, clearing away the inevitable blood spattered, antiseptic scented clutter left over from the operation. She was waiting, she realized, for Dr. Catrell to say something to her. There was no reason why he should. Most doctors weren't aware of the fact that they had lashed out at a nurse, unfairly, or otherwise, during an intricate operation. No doubt, he had forgotten what he had said to her, by now. But he wouldn't have forgotten that she had inadvertently applied too much pressure to the retraction suture. The little misjudgment had become a part of his knowledge of her, and there was no way to erase it from his sharp, doctor's mind. She could only hope that her impression on him had been favorable, otherwise.

Back in the nurse's room with Miss Lucas, Holly slipped out of the wrinkled scrub clothes, and put on her smart, tweed suit, selected with Ocean Breeze in mind. Brian had suggested that she outfit herself for casual living, if she went through with her plan to work in the small, coastal retreat for a few weeks, or months. Until the tourist season ended, she reminded herself, recalling that Dr. Catrell's ad in the Examiner had emphasized his need for a nurse during that particular period.

Miss Lucas slipped back into her starched uniform, regarding Holly with frankly curious eyes. "I can't imagine what a girl like you is doing in Ocean Breeze," Miss Lucas said. "You have big city written all over you. Even in there . . . " she nodded toward the swing door that led to the green tiled surgeries, "I could tell you weren't one of us."

47

Holly glanced up sharply. "Pulling that stay suture loose was a clumsy thing to do," she said. "I've been away from surgery for awhile. But I didn't expect it to show."

"Oh, that," Miss Lucas said, her pouty lips breaking into a smile. "It could have happened to anyone. And you made a good showing for yourself, otherwise. I wouldn't worry about it." The circulation nurse shrugged.

Holly knew that what she said was true. But it hadn't happened to just anyone. It had happened to her. And she *was* worried about it.

"What I meant," Miss Lucas nodded, "is that you look more like a model, than a nurse."

Holly's nimble fingers paused over the gold trimmed buttons on the front of the ascot shirt, as she considered Miss Lucas' remark. A year ago, no one would have made a comment like that about her, she thought. Knowing and working with Brian had made her fashion conscious in a way that she had never been before. She *had* to have nice clothes, to appear with him, circulating among his rich friends, and patients.

"But I am a nurse," she said, after a moment's hesitation, thinking that she had gotten away from that concept of herself, during the months spent in Brian's lavish office. She had been the fashionable girl Brian wanted her to be first, a nurse second. There hadn't been a great deal of satisfaction in the arrangement, if indeed there had been any at all, she told herself, remembering the hours spent under a dryer, in the exclusive stylist's shop on Maiden Lane, or the time spent selecting just the right dress; the proper sports attire; the most attractive uniforms, that hadn't really resembled uniforms at all. Brian had wanted to avoid a sterile, medical look in his office. She had gone to her vague duties there in nylon creations that would not have been permitted inside a G.P.'s office, or a hospital. She'd had to dig in the far corners of her closet to find uniforms to bring with her to Ocean Breeze; the familiar, white starched uniforms she had worn on duty at Mercy, freshly laundered to immaculate crispness.

A new eagerness surged through her. She took a deep breath of the iodoform scented air, and finished buttoning the smart shirt.

"In fact, I intend to be the best nurse Ocean Breeze ever had," she told Miss Lucas impulsively, not minding that her words came out weighted with an idealism she had almost forgotten she possessed. "That's why I'm here. If Dr. Catrell wants me," she added, remembering the O.R. blunder.

She felt a sudden, urgent need to be accepted by the tall gray-eyed doctor, in all of her dedicated capacity as a qualified R.N. She couldn't afford to let her nursing skills deteriorate. Not for Brian, or anyone else. She had worked too hard, for too long, to let that happen.

4

DR CATRELL was waiting for her in the corridor when she finished dressing. The patient, he told her, would be able to go home in a few days, if everything went well. "Pete won't like the idea of Margaret being left alone. We'll be lucky if he doesn't sneak out of the hospital as soon as he comes out of the anesthetic." He didn't mention the incident in surgery.

Holly breathed a little sigh. "Is Les Lenhart really that much of a wolf?" she asked, her slim legs stretching to keep pace with his wide stride.

"Pete Howe seems to think so. At least, where his daughter is concerned," Dr. Catrell said, hooking a comfortable arm through her own to steer her through the heavy, glass door. "Captain will have let her know, by now, what's happened."

51

"Is there someone she can stay with until her father is released from the hospital?" Holly asked.

"Margaret has friends. Girls her own age," Dr. Catrell said. "It isn't as though she were an infant. I imagine it will be up to us to see that she's not left alone tonight."

Us, he had said, as though she belonged. She climbed into the waiting ambulance, beside Joe Green, aware of a sudden, eager throbbing behind her sternum. In the next instant, her eagerness turned to stone, beneath her small round breasts, as she realized that it was possible Dr. Catrell hadn't been including her at all. There was the woman at the motel, where his office was located. It was possible that he had been including her in his 'us'.

She wondered, as the ambulance whipped along the dark, coastal highway, who the woman at the motel might be. Dr. Catrell hadn't mentioned having a wife. But it wasn't impossible. Hardly that, Holly smiled, aware of his vital presence beside her. He was handsome enough, with his crisp, black hair, and storm gray eyes, to charm feminine hearts at will. A man like Dr. Catrell would no doubt have a woman in his life. She had expected that, when she left San Francisco. It was common knowledge that doctors of all ages had long enjoyed a high rating with women. Holly had idolized a few herself, when she was in training.

The ambulance careened around a particularly sharp curve, forcing Dr. Catrell's big, hard body against her own.

"Sorry, Miss Doran," Joe Green said, his coarse voice apologetic. "This highway's a duzy. Lots of wrecks on this road, when the middlewest tourists show up. Those plains people aren't used to our mountains."

"I imagine that keeps you busy, Doctor," Holly said, remembering the frightful bridge accidents, that resulted in strings of screaming ambulances bringing the injured to Mercy. She had helped with her share of those cases. Those who hadn't been D.O.A.

"This stretch of bad road keeps a lot of people in business," Joe Green commented. "Jinx Jones, for instance."

"Jinx is our local junkman," Dr. Catrell explained.

"And Les Lenhart's best friend," Joe Green added. "There's a combination for you. You'll get to know folks, after you've been here awhile, Miss Doran." His tone of voice assumed that she was staying. He hadn't witnessed the slip in O.R.

"Jinx collects metal for a tank and steel outfit in San Francisco," Dr. Catrell said. "He ships it down to them, periodically."

"And makes it pay off," Joe Green said. "It takes money to travel in Les Lenhart's circle. A lot of people in Ocean Breeze can't help wondering how Jinx manages it."

"One of our local mystery men," Dr. Catrell commented. "Jinx, and those hoodlums he hires to help him wreck out the cars he hauls in," Joe Green said. "No one seems to know who they are, or where they come from. But there always seems to be one or two hanging around."

"Transients," Dr. Catrell said. "That's something we get here, during the summer season. There are a few lily fields back in the valleys, where they can pick up a week's work. A few days in Jinx's junkyard is probably a welcome change to some of those kids, after crawling around a five acre garden plucking weeds for days on end. Ocean Breeze is different from your San Francisco, Holly."

"It appeared to be," she said, relishing the sound of her name, spoken in his rich, vibrating voice; liking the gray-eyed doctor, too, wishing he would commit himself about the job. Tell her that he wanted her to stay . . . He had sounded enthusiastic enough, when he met her at the bus-stop cafe. But that was before he had worked with her in surgery. She couldn't be sure herself,

55

that her skill hadn't grown a bit rusty, during the past months. If it had, it was time she was becoming active again; an essential part of medicine as it was practiced by a busy G.P.

★ ★ ★

"We'll stop by Pete's place," Dr. Catrell told her, when the two of them were seated again in his pickup truck. "We'll have to see that Margaret isn't left alone. Pete worries about her enough, as it is."

"Because of Les Lenhart?" Holly asked, thinking that this time, he *had* included her.

"Margaret has a crush on him," Dr. Catrell said, steering the pickup along the gravel road that led into town. "Although her infatuation may fade, when she finds out Les is responsible for her dad's injury."

He turned off of the gravel road, onto the street that followed the harbor shore. Victorian houses, most of them weathered to nondescript shades of gray, looked out over the broad bay. The water, obsidian black in the faint light cast by the street lamps, had become restless in the rising wind. Undulating. The breasts of water, that swelled and came rolling in toward the narrow beach, appeared to be higher than the scraggly hedges that separated the row of houses from the sandy street. A feeling of alarm tugged at Holly.

"Does the water ever swamp the street?" she asked. She had read accounts of storms at sea that sent waves crashing shoreward, to innundate entire communities.

"Occasionally," Dr. Catrell told her. "Once or twice, in the history of this town, these houses have been flooded. The mill was located across the harbor, at one time. A good sized quantity of lumber and some machinery were lost, in one of those soakings. The Lenharts rebuilt at the present site after that happened, although the old buildings are still standing. Jinx Jones uses them for his wrecking business."

The long, low, ramshackle buildings she had seen, when the bus pulled into the small town, Holly thought, isolated on their own jutting bit of land, across the harbor.

"No one here worries a great deal about high water," Dr. Catrell continued. "Just the same, I prefer the headland, Lenhart mansion and all. But people have always been drawn to the sea."

"The primordial instinct," Holly said, a fleeting worry darting across her mind, as she watched the restless, black swells. If there were a tidal wave, or any kind of disaster, where would they take the injured? Seal Beach General was too far, with only one ambulance. She shivered a little, at the thought.

"Cold?" Dr. Catrell asked, feeling her slight trembling. "I was just thinking," she laughed away the cold feeling, that was almost a premonition, drawing her blue gaze away from the undulating, serpentine waters, glad for his warm, confident presence beside her.

"About man seeking the supposed source of his being?" he asked, then continued, before she could give voice to her forebodings. "Pegleg Tom has a different theory. According to him, the men who settled Ocean Breeze were too lazy to haul their building supplies up onto the headland. They had them shipped into the harbor, and piled on the beach, wherever the schooners of their day deposited materials. That accounts for these houses being no more than a stone's throw from the water's edge."

"Pegleg Tom sounds like another local character," Holly stated.

"He is," Dr. Catrell agreed. "He shows up here once or twice a year, and sticks around for a month or so. He's a transient saw sharpener, by trade."

"Does he really have a pegleg?"

"In the best Gold Coast tradition," Dr. Catrell said. "He scorns transportation of any kind. Follows his saw circuit on his mare, and sleeps wherever he can find shelter; under piers, or in the caves below the headlands — a bottle of wine for company, and he's perfectly content."

Holly laughed, amused by the picture Dr. Catrell painted of the old transient, thinking that there was a great deal about Ocean Breeze that was colorful.

"This is Pete Howe's place." He pulled the pickup to a stop before one of the Victorian houses, behind a bright red M.G. "Les Lenhart's car," he told her, throwing open the door, his tan face going suddenly grim.

She climbed out, and followed him to the front door. A quaint door, with a single pane depicting frosty reindeer, she noted, offhandedly, as they waited for someone to answer the bell.

Dr. Catrell pressed the black buzzer again, and a girl's face appeared behind the frosted glass. She opened the door a crack, and peered around the corner of it. Her tawny hair was tousled, her hazel eyes bright. Her lipstick was smudged, to one side of her mouth, giving her a bruised, little girl look.

"Dr. Catrell!" She brushed at her hair with a flutter of her small hand. "How is Daddy? Has something happened . . . ? Les said . . . "

"Pete's going to be fine," Dr Catrell told her. "He'll be in the hospital for awhile. But he's going to be all right."

"I wanted to come, when Captain Lenhart called. But Les came, and he said it wasn't too bad. He said Daddy fell . . . "

Les Lenhart appeared behind Margaret, his strange eyes fiery bright. "Good thing I was there to pull him away from that saw, or it would have cut his leg off," he said. "Margaret needs someone with her tonight," he added, with a clumsy swagger. "I dropped in to keep her company, until she heard . . . "

"Did you tell her how Pete happened to fall into that saw?" Dr. Catrell asked, his gray eyes steady.

"It shook her up enough, without going into the gory details," Les said,

61

his brown jaw setting in a stubborn line.

"What does he mean, Les?" Margaret asked. "Is there something you didn't tell me?"

"What about it, Les?" Dr. Catrell said. "She's going to find out anyway. You may as well be the one to tell her."

"Okay. So I had a little run-in with her old man. It wasn't my fault he melted like an old lady, when I punched him back. He shouldn't have jumped onto me in the first place."

"You mean . . . ?" Margaret Howe's hazel eyes grew round and accusing. "Les! You didn't!"

"Like I said, baby, your old man jumped me. Seems he don't want me hanging around you. Only I've got other ideas."

"Les Lenhart! You're horrid! Horrid!" the girl screamed at him, her pretty face mirroring quick, childish anger. "If I had known . . . " She scrubbed her hand across her smeared lips in what,

Holly knew, with feminine certainty, was an effort to wipe off the feel of Les Lenhart's knowing mouth. "I don't ever want to see you again, Les Lenhart."

"We'll see about that, baby," Les said. He turned and slammed out the door, leaving the frosted reindeer, and Margaret, quivering behind him.

"Les lied to me," Margaret said, wiping at her eyes. "Didn't Captain . . . ?" Holly began.

"Captain wouldn't have told her," Dr. Catrell said, before she could finish. "Les is still a Lenhart, no matter what he's done." He turned to Margaret. "I want you to get some things together. I'm taking you out to the motel."

"Does Gen know?" Margaret asked.

"She won't mind," Dr. Catrell told her. "Business hasn't picked up yet, for the summer, so there's plenty of room. And she'll welcome a guest." He glanced at Holly. "Two guests," he revised the statement. "I had Gen fix up one of the motel units for you, Miss

Doran. I think you'll be comfortable."

She wanted to ask who Gen was, knowing, even as the question flitted through her mind, that he was speaking of the voluptuous, long-haired woman who had run out into the wind to tell him about Pete Howe.

The wind clutched at Holly's soft, dark hair when she climbed out of the truck in front of the motel, pulling a silken strand from her neat French roll, and ruffling the delicate curls at the nape of her neck.

"The wind always gives me the creeps," Margaret huddled close, prying at Holly's arm with nervous fingers. "Would you mind if I spent the night in your room, Miss Doran?"

"Of course not," Holly told the girl.

"I like you," Margaret Howe stated, with disarming frankness. "I hope you stay in Ocean Breeze a long time."

"I do, too," Holly heard herself saying.

Dr. Catrell seemed not to have heard, as he fitted a key into a lock, and threw open the door to one of the units. "I'll be right next door, if you need anything," he said. "We'll discuss the job in the morning." He turned and hurried off toward his office.

Gen wasn't his wife, then, Holly thought, stepping into the room, remembering that Gen had emerged from a door farther down the row. It shouldn't make any difference to her, whether Dr. Catrell were married, or not, Holly told herself. She wasn't yet certain that he still wanted her. And even if he did, his marital status would have no bearing on her presence in his headland office.

The motel unit she and Margaret Howe had entered had been a double. One of the two sleeping rooms had been converted into a sitting room, made cozy with bright flowered drapes, and a couch covered with a matching slip-cover. Geraniums bloomed on a window shelf, and a comfortable looking chair occupied one corner.

"Wow! Gen did it up brown for

you," Margaret voiced her approval, dipping into a candy dish, popping one of the mints between her pink lips. "Les should see this. Although I doubt if he'd be impressed." She seemed to have forgotten her anger at the youngest of the Lenhart sons.

"Why Les?" Holly couldn't resist asking.

"Captain built this motel for him," Margaret explained. "Les wasn't interested in the mill the way Karl is."

"Les doesn't seem to be the type to manage a motel," Holly said, stepping into the bedroom, seeing that the same magic touch had been employed there to give it a homey, lived-in look.

"Captain found that out the hard way," Margaret said. "There was some kind of scandal. Daddy won't tell me the details, and it happened before I was old enough to know about things like . . . like that," she ended lamely. "It had something to do with Gen. She's lived here for as long as I can remember."

"Les Lenhart hardly seems that old," Holly said.

"You don't think about age, with Les," Margaret said. "He's pretty old, I guess. But he's one of those types. You know. Perpetually young. All of the girls at school are crazy to date him. Nobody else around here has a real honest-to-goodness yacht. Besides, Les is exciting." Margaret suddenly yawned. "Golly, Miss Doran. I'm sleepy, now that I know Daddy's going to be all right."

"So am I," Holly told the girl, reaching to turn back the twin beds. The linens emanated a dainty, lavender fragrance. Someone had gone to a great deal of effort to transform the impersonal surroundings into a liveable apartment, Holly thought. She felt an eagerness to meet the women named Gen.

"'Night," Margaret murmured, crawling into her own bed, her hazel eyes closing at once.

Holly lay awake, in spite of the fact

that she was dead tired. She tried to focus her thoughts on Brian, and found herself thinking about Dr. Key Catrell, instead. She wanted more than a scolding from the tall, handsome man who looked like a deck hand, and who, she admitted to herself, had stirred something that lay deep inside of her, like a seed ready to burst forth with new life.

She wouldn't go back to Brian, she thought, even if Dr. Catrell decided he couldn't use her. She would apply for a job at Seal Beach General. Hospitals were always on the lookout for R.N.'s.

She finally dozed, a determined little smile quirking her ripe lips.

5

HOLLY awakened to the fragrant aroma of coffee, the following morning. She opened her eyes to see a red-haired woman standing beside her bed. The woman wore white, like a nurse. For a brief instant, while she hovered in that hazy, phantom state between sleep and wakefulness, she imagined that she was back at Mercy Hospital.

The red-haired person hovering over her had full breasts under the crisp white uniform, and a tapered waist that shelved into broad hips. Gen! The events of the previous day focused in her mind with sudden clarity. She sat up in bed, her dark hair, freed of the French roll, tumbling around her sleep-softened face. She glanced over to see that Margaret's bed was empty.

"She got up early to go to Seal Beach

with Key," the woman said. "I thought you might be in the shower, when you didn't answer my knock. So I let myself in. By the way, I'm Gen Byrde. I run the cafe, and manage the motel for Key . . . Dr. Catrell. You're Holly Doran," she stated. Then, "K . . . Dr. Catrell told me." She turned to put the tray she carried on the bedside table.

"This is kind of you." Holly smiled her appreciation. "I certainly didn't expect to have my early morning coffee in bed."

"Dr. Catrell ordered it for you." She didn't stumble over his name, this time, in an effort to avoid familiarity. "You'll have to come over to the cafe for your bacon and eggs. Dr. Catrell arranged for me to give you your meals, free of charge. *If* you stay." There was a reserved air about the woman, who, Holly thought, was actually no more than three or four years older than herself. Gen Byrde's green eyes, faded a little from too much seeing and knowing, beneath full lids, and her full, ripe body, gave an impression of mature womanhood that belied the youthful smoothness of her unlined face.

"I hope I will be staying," Holly said, wanting to be friendly toward this woman who shared Dr. Catrell's life here on the headland, in a manner that was not yet clear to her. Holly sensed resentment, barely concealed beneath the voluptuous woman's soft, ripe exterior.

There wasn't time, now, to worry about who or what the bright-haired woman was to Key Catrell, M.D. She hurried into the shower, after Gen had gone, eager for her interview with Ocean Breeze's handsome, gray-eyed doctor. She let the cold spray sting her skin, until it had taken on a rosy glow, then stepped out to towel herself.

She brushed her long, dark tresses, and coiled the silken length expertly into a French roll, that rode high on her head. It made the perfect setting for the proud, black-banded nurse's cap she perched on top of the shining topknot, with an impulsive little gesture that defied the indecision she felt.

The wind that had raced across the headland with such terrific force the night before, had quieted. A low-hanging bank of fog hung over the outside world, so thick and moist that it frosted Holly's hair, as she hurried across the motel driveway, to the steamy-windowed little cafe. Gen Byrde was alone, inside, frying crisp, fragrant bacon at the grill behind the counter, when she glanced up to see Holly enter. At one end of the counter, a radio blared the morning news.

"Key should be back soon," Gen said, above the precise tones of the newscaster's voice. She turned a guarded smile on Holly. "Dr. Catrell, to you," she added, her jade-green eyes inscrutable, beneath their heavy lids.

Holly climbed onto one of the red upholstered stools, thinking that there was a casual possessiveness in the way the red-haired woman spoke of the handsome, Ocean Breeze doctor. As though she had some special claim on him . . . And she very well could, Holly conceded, living in the motel, as she did, managing that particular segment of his affairs. For no reason, the thought displeased her.

She ate the breakfast Gen set before her in silence, cutting up the crisp bacon, popping it between her ripe lips. She would have enjoyed talking to Gen Byrde. But the cafe manageress had disappeared into the kitchen that opened off of the tiny room, almost as though she wanted to avoid her, Holly thought, hoping the woman's chilly attitude would give way to a more natural friendliness, *if* she stayed.

Dr. Catrell hadn't returned, by the time she finished her breakfast. She stepped out into the cool, misty air, just as a car pulled off of the highway, and stopped in front of Dr. Catrell's office. A girl in her mid twenties, her body distended with pregnancy, slid from behind the wheel of the long, black vehicle, that looked surprisingly rich, for Ocean Breeze tastes.

First patient of the day, Holly thought, feeling an excitement that she hadn't known since she left Mercy to work for Brian. She hurried to open the office door, finding that Dr. Catrell had left it unlocked, and taking it upon herself to escort the pregnant woman inside. There was a note for her, scrawled hurriedly on the back of a page from a prescription pad. *Back at nine*, it read. *Prep Louise Lenhart — if she comes. If she doesn't, call and remind her of her appointment.*

Holly read it. And read it again, her breath catching in her throat. He had accepted her, then, without question. And, because she had been afraid that he would no longer want her, after that slip in surgery, and had worried about it, a sudden little twinge of anger came alive in her. He had taken a great deal for granted, she told herself.

Then, as suddenly as it had grown, the feeling gave way to pride. He had counted on her to report for duty, and to begin preparations for the day, without any further ado. Brian, she couldn't help thinking, as she bustled about, making herself familiar with her new surroundings, would have demanded a list of references a mile long. There were other considerations, too, that would have concerned him; salary, for instance. She wouldn't quibble about it. Her room, and the meals Dr. Catrell had arranged would count for something. Brian, if he were here, would be horrified at the mere idea of such casual arrangements. He had paid her a fabulous sum, each month, for doing practically nothing. She stifled the thought, glancing at the patient.

"Mrs. Lenhart?" she asked.

Louise Lenhart's face had grown full, with her pregnancy, giving her the expression of an indulged child. Holly hoped Mrs. Lenhart wasn't as spoiled and pampered as she appeared to be, thinking that she must be Karl's wife, as she showed her along the corridor to a door marked 'one'. She pushed it open, saw that it was an examination room, and showed Louise Lenhart inside.

She noticed, with a nurse's keen perception, as she assisted the pregnant woman with her clothes — expensive clothes, with a Jax label — that Mrs. Lenhart's fingers and ankles were slightly puffy.

"How far along are you?" she asked, her voice friendly, softly reassuring.

"Five months," Louise Lenhart told her.

Holly bit back a little gasp. Five months! And the woman looked big enough to be delivered within a week. She spread the sheet across Mrs. Lenhart's legs, permitting her to sit up, while she wrapped the sphygmomanometer cuff around her arm — an arm that was slightly swollen, Holly noted — to take a B.P.R. Her trained eyes didn't miss the flush that arose to Louise Lenhart's cheeks, as she slipped the tips of the Y shaped stethoscope into her ears, and listened for the familiar crackling sounds that indicated the contraction of the ventricles; the force of blood being pushed against artery walls. The patient's heart had set up a terrific pounding. Rapid pulse, Holly categorized the sound, her blue gaze concentrated on the mercury tube, her own heart racing, as her eyes tabulated the systolic reading recorded there. 180, when it shouldn't have been more than 120. 130, at the very most!

"How long has it been since the Doctor saw you?" she asked quietly, rerolling the rubbery, gray cuff.

"Three months, or so," Louise told her casually. "I haven't been back since. Mother wanted me to visit her, before I got too big to travel. You're the nurse who helped Key put Pete Howe back together last night," she added, suddenly, tipping her head to one side, looking at Holly as though she were seeing her for the first time.

"I'm Miss Doran," Holly said. "I expect to be working with Dr. Catrell for awhile."

"Les described you at breakfast," Louise Lenhart said. "You made quite an impression. Every pretty girl does. I did, myself, once, before I took on the unattractive dimensions of a prehistoric tadpole." She smoothed a wistful hand across her swollen abdomen. "Les and I are birds of a feather. We both hate that old house. Not that it does either of us any good." She shrugged her shoulders. "I talk too much," she said, cutting herself off abruptly.

Holly left her, wondering if Louise had any idea that her pregnancy had become dangerously complicated. Bordering on pre-eclampsia, Holly categorized the symptoms automatically.

★ ★ ★

Dr. Key Catrell arrived at the office promptly at nine. "Good morning." He greeted Holly with a broad smile, his gray eyes alive with interest and enthusiasm.

Not like Brian's grumbly, early morning demeanor, she couldn't help making the comparison. Brian was a nocturnal type, by his own admission, arranging as many appointments as possible for the late afternoon and evening hours, mixing business with pleasure, on more than one occasion, and without any obvious qualms.

She picked up Louise Lenhart's card, and handed it to him. "Everything is ready," she said. "How is Pete Howe? And Margaret?"

"Pete's coming home in a day or two. He can't bear to be away from Margaret, so I relented, although he'll have to stay off of that leg. And our Azalea Queen is safely in school today," he added. "She'll be busy taking care of Pete in her spare hours, when he comes home. I told her I was counting on her to play the role of nurse. She wants to go into training, when she graduates. Probably because she likes the uniform, if I know Margaret."

"A lot of young girls are dazzled by a white uniform," Holly said. "I was, myself, before I grew up. When I finally reached maturity, I knew it was more than the privilege of wearing a white uniform, that I wanted. Margaret will grow up, too," she added, with a purely feminine little smile.

"I hope so," Dr. Catrell said. "I doubt if Pete has told her where babies come from yet. He's overly protective of the girl. She may change her mind about nursing — and Les Lenhart — when she discovers what life is really about."

"She's a sweet girl," Holly said. "If . . . the wrong man turns her head, it could spoil what she has. Those intangible qualities that made her this town's beauty queen. Her naiveté is a part of it. A person worries about a girl like Margaret."

A bright look flashed into Dr. Catrell's gray eyes, startling her, causing her to wonder what she had said to strike such a response. "You mean that, don't you," he said, his eyes alive with flecks of golden light that turned them as lucid as a child's. "I have a confession to make. I had some half-scared notion that a city nurse, who's accustomed to the frills and excitement of big time medicine, might not want to involve herself, the way a nurse — and a doctor — has to become involved, in order to give these people the best possible service." He paused, a thoughtful look crossing his face. "It takes an old-fashioned element, something I can only define as the personal touch. The old family doctors, who set up a practice in their kitchen, and took time to listen to everyone's troubles, had it." His gray eyes held her own. "I'm glad you're the kind of girl who can worry about Margaret, Miss Doran. Holly . . . Do you mind?"

"Not at all," she said, thinking that he hadn't been concerned about the slip she had made in O.R. at all. It had been her big city background, and appearance.

"I'm glad I found you here, when I came in just now," he said, his gaze shifting to rove the length of her figure, chic in the starched uniform, moving upward to rest with frank approval on the pert, black-banded cap. "I always was partial to women in white." He turned on his heel, to disappear into the lavatory at the end of the hall, leaving her standing there, tingling with a rare pleasure.

The feeling stayed with her, as she moved about the small, clean office, involving a part of her that was all woman; all longing, with a yearning that Dr. Brian Merdahl had not, with all of his suave utterances of love, been quite able to satisfy. Rather, Brian had frightened her, with his sophisticated persistence and persuasion. He had accused her of not knowing what she wanted, when she shrank from his demanding kisses. She wondered, as she followed Dr. Catrell down the narrow hallway, if Brian would miss her. Most likely, he wouldn't, she conceded, with Felicia Onstott ready and willing to console him. The thought didn't particularly worry her. And it should, she told herself, if she really cared . . .

She stood by, while Dr. Catrell examined Louise Lenhart, assisting him with the draping, reassuring the pregnant woman by her mere, starched, female presence. Dr. Catrell finished the examination, handing the speculum to Holly, to be rinsed, and put into the small autoclave. His face had grown stern; his gray eyes dark. He reached for one of Mrs. Lenhart's hands, and let it rest in his broad palm, looking at it, pressing his thumb into the swollen flesh, to test the tension of the drawn skin.

"Why did you wait so long to come back?" he asked, his husky voice quietly effective.

"Mother wanted me to visit her, before I got too big to travel," she repeated the excuse she had given Holly.

"There are M.D.'s in Tucson," Dr. Catrell scolded. "But that's beside the point. If you'll recall, I specifically told you not to plan any long trips, without talking to me, first."

"How do you know I didn't see a doctor in Tucson?" Louise Lenhart tilted her sleek head to one side, squinting her eyes defiantly.

"No reputable doctor would have permitted you to get into this condition," Dr. Catrell told her. "You've gained ten pounds over the maximum gain for your entire pregnancy, and you still have three months to go."

"I have a tendency to put on weight," Louise shrugged, her round face growing flushed, a blue vein starting to pound in her temple. Holly hated to think what her B.P.R. might be at the precise moment.

"You've been using salt, too, of course. I can tell," he added, before Louise could utter a denial. "What happened to the diet I recommended? Now you'll not have any, and you aren't going to like it."

"I can't say that I particularly like anything about this pregnancy," Louise sparred. "It's a nuisance. If I'd known beforehand, that it would be like this . . . " She shrugged again.

"It doesn't have to be a nuisance. Nor does it have to run into trouble, which is exactly what will happen if you don't start caring for yourself properly," Dr. Catrell told her bluntly. "Your blood pressure is the next thing to get out of control, now. This time, I'm not merely telling you what I want you to do, if you expect me to continue caring for you. I'm going to write out a list of orders, on the premise that seeing it set down on paper will make it easier. I want you to wait here, until they're ready." He turned to Holly. "Make an appointment for Mrs. Lenhart, for a week from today."

"But that's so soon, Key," Louise Lenhart said. "I . . . Oh well."

"We're going to have trouble when that baby comes, if that girl doesn't do better," Dr. Catrell told Holly, when they had left the pregnant woman alone to dress.

Mere minutes later, Louise Lenhart's orders were ready, neatly stapled to the diet sheet Dr. Catrell had given her. Holly hurried into 'one' with them, hoping that they weren't wasted effort on Dr. Catrell's part. Toxemia — that peculiar kind of blood poisoning that occurs only during pregnancy — could develop in a matter of days, if Louise kept on as she had been.

She pushed open the door, eager to caution the woman, once more. No doctor wanted to care for a patient who refused to care for herself. She cut the thought short, catching her breath. The examining room was empty. Louise Lenhart had gone! Holly hurried back down the corridor, to the waiting room. There was no sign of her there, among the four patients who had come in, while she and Dr.

Catrell had been busy. Her blue gaze flew to the window, and saw that the long, black car was gone from the space in front of the office. Dr. Catrell had asked the pregnant girl to wait, and she had deliberately flaunted him, by walking out!

Holly concealed her irritation from the waiting patients, with a bright, professional smile. She would have to tell Dr. Catrell what had happened. Most likely, he would be more discouraged than ever with his patient. She went back to his office, and laid the stapled sheets on the big desk, before turning to search for case histories in the surprisingly crammed file. She found them, and went to call the next patients back.

Guy Kessler, an oldish man — sixty-two, his card said — with an inguinal hernia. A woman suffering from hypertension. And a tall, teenager, named Terry Williams, who exhibited symptoms that could be anything, from a mild cold, to infectious mononucleosis.

Dr. Catrell suspected the latter, when he examined the boy half an hour later, and found that he had been experiencing tiredness for a time; that the lymph nodes in the sides of his neck were swollen; the spleen enlarged.

"We'll run a test to confirm it," he told Holly. "It may be too early to detect a heterophile antibody. But we'll know, if the test reveals an abundance of conomytes."

The too-many white cells were there, teeming in the boy's blood, when Holly made the test.

"This means plenty of rest for you, son," Dr. Catrell told the boy.

"I ain't got time to rest," Terry Williams told him, his lean, teenage face sullen. He wore his hair long. Rod-style, Holly thought, remembering the young hoodlums who found their way into Mercy. The boy could easily have come from San Francisco's North Beach, if appearances meant anything.

"I'm afraid you're going to have to find time, if you want to throw off those bugs," Dr. Catrell told him.

"I can see me gettin' rest in that grubby trailer, with a half dozen brats under foot," the boy said, his voice bitter. "Something like this would have to happen, just when I land me a good job. I shouldn't have come here. I wouldn't have, if Ma hadn't made me. She was scared I had something the brats would catch. If they get sick, she'll have to take off work to take care of them."

"Who takes care of them, now?" Dr. Catrell asked.

The boy gave him a suspicious look. "You ain't fixin' to turn Ma in, are you Doc?" he said. "They tried to take the kids away from Ma, last place we was. We had to move on."

"Just making conversation," Dr. Catrell said. He glanced at Holly. "Chloramphenicol, nurse."

The recently developed antibiotic, Holly knew, would, in most cases, control the infection. But the boy would still need rest.

"Hey, Doc," Terry Williams was saying. "Is that one of those wonder drugs, like penicillin, or aureomycin?" His brown eyes lost their belligerent look, showing interest.

Dr. Catrell smiled at the boy, nodding. "You seem to know your medicine," he commented.

"Dig this, Doc," Terry said, with a bitter little laugh. "When I was a brat, I dreamed of being a somebody, like you, stethoscope, hypodermic needles. The works. Ma even raked together enough coins to get me one of them little doctor kits."

"That sounds like a worthwhile dream," Dr. Catrell said. "You're still young, Terry."

"Don't try to kid me, Doc. What chance have I got of ever gettin' educated, with Ma and the kids to take care of. I'm lucky to be doctorin' cars."

"Doctoring cars?" Dr. Catrell gave him a startled look.

"I'm workin' for Jinx Jones," the

boy said. "Patching together wrecks. We lose a few patients, same as you, Doc." He laughed harshly at his own little joke.

"Don't you suppose he has a father somewhere?" Holly asked, when Terry Williams had gone. "Someone who could help out?"

"The facts of life preclude the father bit," Dr. Catrell told her, with a grin. "Seriously, it would have only embarrassed the boy to inquire into that aspect of his life. Most of these women who travel through with a batch of kids, working their way from one bean patch to the next, don't have a man, legally, or otherwise. In most cases, the husband has deserted them, and they haven't the slightest idea where he is. Or there never was a husband," he added. "But that doesn't keep the kids from coming."

"You'd think they'd do something," Holly said, thinking that the plight of such people seemed so hopeless.

"They can't afford to," Dr. Catrell

said. "Women like Terry's mother are lonely. They snatch at what happiness they can, where they find it, and worry about the consequences later, or not at all."

"Terry seems to be a bright boy." She picked up the card Dr. Catrell had filled out on him, to return it to the files. "It seems a shame that a young man like that has to be denied, because his mother has wanderlust."

"I agree." Dr. Catrell nodded his crisp, dark head. "Terry has brains enough to know that he's throwing his life away. And ambition enough, if I don't miss my guess, to try to do something about it. A doctor has to have confidence in people, or he'd be tempted to throw in the sponge," he added, his gray eyes intense.

"I hadn't ever thought about it like that," she admitted, thinking that it was true. A doctor — and a nurse, for that matter — did what he or she could for a patient. But whether or not their efforts were worthwhile, beyond the narrow scope of satisfaction a medical team derived from applying their skills successfully, remained entirely up to the individual.

She hadn't actually *had* to think, in Brian's office. No wonder she had been so vague about her 'true self', as Brian put it. Perhaps now that she was here, with this clear-eyed, concerned doctor, all of that would change.

6

THE rest of the day flew by quickly. Guy Kessler, at Dr. Catrell's suggestion, decided on surgery for his hernia.

"I don't want to frighten you, Guy," Dr. Catrell told him. "But as bad as that thing is getting, you could end up with a strangulation. You'll wish you'd let Dr. Piercey operate twenty years ago, after it's all over." He glanced at Holly. "Call Seal Beach General. Schedule Mr. Kessler for next Monday morning."

"Now that I've made up my mind, how about waiting until after the Azalea Festival," Guy Kessler said. He was a single man, balding, his myopic eyes enlarged behind thick lenses. He was also Ocean Breeze's chief of police. "We're going to have a lot of activity here, during the next few weeks. I guess I can let you in on this, Doc, since nobody said it had to be kept secret." His enlarged eyes grew shrewd. "There's been a report that a ring of car thieves is operating somewhere here on the coast. The California authorities found a stolen car, just over the line, that had been headed this way. Abandoned," he added. "An all points bulletin came through, to keep an eye out for suspicious looking characters. With something like that brewing, I want to stick pretty close to the job."

"This thing will wait that long, if you're careful," Dr. Catrell said. "And if you think it's necessary," he added.

"I know Ocean Breeze, isn't a likely hangout for criminals," Guy Kessler told him. "But you never know. Especially with the element Jinx Jones and Les Lenhart attract. Anyone of their chums could pass for a hoodlum, not to mention the fruit tramps that pass through here."

"There'd be some problem of disposing of stolen cars, in a community this size," Dr. Catrell reasoned. "With only one road running through town, the operators of a big time ring would be taking quite a chance."

"The authorities have a strong suspicion that the cars are being shipped out of the country," Guy Kessler's voice was confidential. "That means that the coastal town serving as their disposal center has to have a harbor. Ocean Breeze qualifies on that score. I'll admit not many ships put in here," he added. "The lumber barges that haul Lenhart's redwood down the coast. And that rusty old tub that picks up Jinx's scrap."

"From the look of the junk piled around those old buildings he occupies, I'd say it's bringing in scrap, rather than hauling it out," Dr. Catrell remarked. "Those junk heaps never seem to go down."

"It's always that way with junk." Guy Kessler's aging face took on a sagacious look. "Thank goodness the old mill site is located across the harbor, away from town. I'm afraid tourists wouldn't be much impressed with that particular kind of scenery. That pier over there should be condemned. It would be, if it didn't belong to Les Lenhart."

The police chief left the office, an important little swagger making his middle-aged body seem almost youthful. "Guy hasn't had anything this important to occupy his mind in all the years he's served this community," Dr. Catrell said. "It'd really give his ego a lift, if he *could* catch those car thieves."

★ ★ ★

The office was miraculously empty, by noon, and Dr. Catrell escorted Holly across the blacktop parking space to Gen Byrde's small, neat cafe. They sat side by side on the high counter stools, inhaling the mouth watering aroma of the day's special.

"One of the reasons I bought this place was because Gen went with it,"

97

Dr. Catrell told Holly. "Best eating place on the coast."

"Margaret told me Gen has been here a long time, according to a teenage girl's reckoning," Holly said.

"Is that all Margaret told you?"

"She said something about Captain Lenhart having built this place for Les. And a scandal of some kind," she added daringly, not quite certain that she should bring *that* up.

"There's been more than one scandal, where Les is concerned." Dr. Catrell's voice remained calm. "His escapades have become so old hat, the town doesn't take notice any more. And it should." He cut himself off short, as Gen Byrde came to take their order.

The voluptuous redhead busied herself behind the counter, preparing salads; laying hot, light rolls on a plate. She would have to wait until sometime when Gen Byrde wasn't around, to find out more about Les Lenhart's escapades, Holly decided, thinking that it was only natural for Margaret

Howe to find the fiery-eyed, blond man so attractive; wondering, in the next breath, why women were so often drawn to a man who flaunted convention.

She couldn't help wondering, too, about Gen Byrde. The woman had the kind of bold, voluptuous looks that drew male eyes like a magnet. She was warm and friendly toward the male customers who came into the small cafe, joking with them in a light, easy manner that made them laugh. One of them playfully slapped her firm rump, when she darted from behind the counter to serve the two small tables beneath the geranium bright windows. Their male laughter gave the place a slightly ribald air that filled Holly with an unexpected nostalgia for the big dining room at Mercy, where interns and nurses mingled to exchange hospital gossip.

Dr. Catrell seemed not to notice the by-play, concentrating his attention on the delicious food Gen set before them, and on Holly's bright, pretty face, when she made a remark about the pleasant, friendly atmosphere of the cafe. "Gen's a friendly girl," he said, noncommittally. "I've given her strict orders to see that you're comfortable here with us. Now that I've lured you up here, I don't want you running back to San Francisco."

"I don't think I'll be doing that, Doctor. At least, not for awhile," she added, thinking of Brian. She had to be very certain of her feelings for Dr. Brian Merdahl, when she did go back, she thought. The idea of returning to him frightened her a little. She felt much more comfortable here with this white shirted, denim clad, headland doctor.

There was the usual assortment of patients waiting, when Holly and Dr. Catrell finished lunch. The afternoon flew by so quickly, that it was over before Holly realized it. She found Dr. Catrell seated at his big desk when she went in to put the final straightening touches on the office that evening. He picked up the stapled sheets Louise Lenhart had left behind, as she entered. "Thank goodness, they aren't all like her," he said.

"What are you going to do about her?" Holly asked.

"Hope that she follows the orders I gave her, without this," he said, tapping a spatulate finger against the piece of paper. "We'll see how she is, next week. If she hasn't made some progress toward getting her weight and that swelling down, I'll talk to Karl." With that, he slammed the drawer of his desk closed, on the neglected sheets, and unfolded his long frame from the hinged, oak chair. "Now, how about dinner? Afterward, we can take a circle through town, if you don't mind my ratty old pickup. A grand tour of all points of interest."

He was trying to be kind, she knew, by the look in his fabulous gray eyes. She accepted, thinking that he might not be so generous, after the novelty of having a nurse on the premises wore off. Doctors developed a blind spot for the women in white who worked beside them day in and day out. An efficient nurse sometimes found herself being categorized as standard medical equipment.

She slipped out of her uniform, determined not to think of Brian, this night. The day had been a busy one — the busiest she had known since she left Mercy. It would feel good to relax beside Dr. Key Catrell, over one of Gen Byrde's delicious meals, letting his rich, husky voice soothe away her tiredness.

7

THE fog, that had hung low over the headland when Holly had awakened that morning, was gone, burned out by the spring sun that had broken through by eleven o'clock to lavish its warm rays on the fragrant, coastal greenery. The lush fragrance of azaleas, as fiery red as the soft, silk blouse Holly had chosen to top her white, pleated skirt, greeted her nostrils as she stepped out of her comfortable rooms into a blazing sunset. Dr. Catrell offered her his hand — and she took it, as naturally as though she had been doing it all of her life, to walk beside him to the small cafe.

An assortment of customers, most of them male, was there before them, lined along the counter. They turned disinterestedly, at the sound of the door opening, the expression in their eyes changing noticeably, at the sight of Holly's fresh, wholesome loveliness.

"No need to ask them whether or not they approve of my new R.N.," Dr. Catrell said, under his breath. "I want you to know that I do, too, in case you didn't get the message." She looked up to see his storm-gray eyes frank with admiration.

"Thank you, Doctor," she told him, feeling a flush rising above the neckline of the silk blouse, to concentrate in two burning spots on her freshly scrubbed cheeks.

"You two are late," Gen called to them, drawing his attention away from her. "I thought you weren't coming."

"I always have," Dr. Catrell said. "There's no reason why I should change my habits now." Flecks of patient amusement lighted his gray eyes.

"I thought maybe things might be different, now," Gen said, her jade-green eyes resting significantly on Holly.

The woman was jealous of her,

Holly thought. That explained her aloof manner. Did it mean that there was something between Dr. Catrell and this knowing, voluptuous woman? The thought ached in her throat, forming a harsh, little lump. She swallowed hard, aware of the murmur of male voices surrounding them. She knew the men were talking about her. She could feel their eyes on her, as she stood beside Dr. Catrell. He glanced down at her. "This place is too crowded. How about taking some trays to your place, if it's not an imposition?"

"It's not," she said hurriedly, wanting to get out of the cafe, away from the customers' knowing eyes, and Gen's jade-green glare.

"Do you think you can trust him?" Gen Byrde said. Sudden ribald laughter filled the tiny room.

"You should know, Gen," one of the men at the counter said. There was more laughter. Gen, unexpectedly, joined in the rude mirth, seemingly unperturbed by the coarse remark, her green eyes unchanging above the ripe curve of her mouth.

Holly felt her face flush with color. She looked up at Key Catrell, and saw, with a surging sense of relief, that he *wasn't* laughing. She nodded her shiny, dark head. "Yes, I think I'd like that, Doctor," she said quietly.

Minutes later, Gen shoved loaded trays across the counter toward them. They had started toward the door, when it flew open, and a blond giant of a man stepped through it, blocking their path. Les Lenhart! Surprisingly, Holly's heart beat faster at the sight of his broad-shouldered ruggedness. No wonder Margaret, with her limited experience, considered him a god of sorts. He *was* striking, in a way that few men were. Not handsome, like Dr. Catrell — and Brian. But *unusual*, Holly thought, aware of his bright eyes on her, burning along her trim figure, luscious in the red silk, and white pleats.

He stepped aside, reluctantly, to let

them pass, when Dr. Catrell moved toward him. "You going to add that one to your collection, Les?" someone behind them asked, before the swinging door cut off the sound of his voice.

"What do you think?" Les replied, his voice cocky.

"I hope you don't mind my inviting myself in on you like this." Dr. Catrell seemed not to have heard.

"Not at all." She let him help her with her tray, while she opened the door to her motel room, stepping inside and turning to invite him in.

It was pleasant in the living room, although there were some changes she wanted to make — if she stayed that long, Holly amended the thought. Changes that would reflect her own personality, rather than Gen Byrde's. But, for now, it was homelike, and comfortable.

"This looks good," Dr. Catrell said, placing his tray beside hers on the coffee table, sinking into the low couch, and reaching to set it on tall knees.

There was a light rap on the door, before they could begin. It was Gen, bearing one of the glass percolators filled with steaming coffee. "One cup won't be enough," she said, depositing it on the table. Her green eyes flicked across Holly, seated across from the Doctor, in the room's only overstuffed chair. Holly had the distinct feeling that the red-haired woman had come to spy on them. She must let Gen know, someway, at breakfast the following morning, that she was engaged. It would put both of their minds at ease.

Everything about the dinner was delicious, Holly thought later, when they had finished the final crumbs of Dutch chocolate cake, and poured the last fragrant drop from the coffee pot. Dr. Catrell carried the trays back to the cafe, while she freshened her lipstick, and slipped into a sweater for the ride into town.

"Let's get away from here, before the phone rings," he grinned, when she emerged from her bedroom. "I'm enjoying this too much to be interrupted again. I did tell Gen where we're going, though, just in case," he added, ruefully. "So if you see someone run out waving a white banner at us, as we roll regally through town, don't be alarmed. It will be my answering service getting in touch."

Holly laughed, feeling suddenly gay, as she went with him out into the tangy, salt-tainted evening, thinking that it was good to be venturing into strange places with a man. A *new* man, she thought wickedly, remembering Brian. A man who seemed as enthusiastic as herself. Brian had always worn a bored, man-of-the-world expression, when they went out together, as though he had seen it all, and there was nothing left that could excite him.

The last rays of sunlight had disappeared from the glimmering, dark sheath of water. Holly snuggled the fluffy sweater up around her chin, shivering a little with pure delight, as the truck swung out onto Highway

101. Lights flashed on in the upper story of the Lenhart mansion, as they drove by, barely visible through the screening limbs of twisted spruce.

"That looks like a dreary place to rear a child," Holly said.

"I agree." Dr. Catrell glanced toward her, his gray eyes smiling. "It's more like a museum than a home, with all of Captain's model ships sitting around."

They turned onto a narrow, unpaved street, that followed the sandy shore toward the crashing breakers beyond the broad bay mouth. The long, crouching buildings of the old mill were barely visible across the harbor. Holly made out the bulky outline of a ship, docked at the rickety pier that jutted out from the dark heaps of scrap. Jinx Jones wrecking business looked like a losing proposition, in spite of what Joe Green had said about the young owner traveling in Les Lenhart's circle.

Lenhart and Sons lumber mill was something else again. The big, new mill, upriver, sparkled with fresh paint and prosperity. "Thanks to Karl Lenhart's able management," Dr. Catrell told Holly, when she commented on the contrast. "Les owns the old mill site. Captain deeded it to him, when he failed with the motel. Les rents it to Jinx, I suppose, which may be the reason they've become friends." He turned the pickup onto the stretch of beach, and cut the motor.

A passageway had been dredged through the sandbar, at the river's mouth, and a lumber barge, piled high with redwood, was being towed out to sea by a tug that looked like a mere toy, compared to the monstrous load trailing behind it.

"I wouldn't believe it, if I hadn't seen it with my own eyes," Holly smiled.

"In the good old days, they hauled the lumber out by schooner," Dr. Catrell told her. "Captain Lenhart stood at the wheel of one of them, himself. That's where he came by the name."

"It must have been an exciting life."

Holly's blue eyes scanned the harbor, admiring the graceful lines of the vessels that bobbed against the trim, white outline of Les Lenhart's yacht.

"Captain is still crazy about seacraft," Dr. Catrell said. "It must be tough on him to have a yacht in the family, and never set foot on it."

"Doesn't he go out with Les?"

Dr. Catrell shook his head, slipping a long arm casually along the back of the seat. "Captain made a vow, when Mrs. Lenhart was drowned, that he'd never again set foot aboard a boat. He's stuck to it."

"Les and Karl's mother?"

Dr. Catrell nodded. "Captain felt responsible for her death. She hated boats, as much as he loves them. The story goes that he forced her to go out with him, in a little salmon rigger he bought to fool around with, as a hobby. He had some idea that she could overcome her fear of the water, if she grew to know it. You know the old maxim. We only fear the unknown . . . At any rate, a storm came up and the boat capsized. Ruby Lenhart was in the cabin, huddled on the bunk, her face buried in blankets. They found her like that, when the remains of the boat washed ashore."

"How awful!"

"Captain's kept his word about not setting foot on another boat. But he still loves them as much as ever. There are models in every room of that old mansion. It's an obsession really."

"What about Les? Does he share his father's interest?"

"To the extent that he enjoys cruising around on that fancy bauble out there." He pointed toward the yacht, that swayed gracefully with the surge of the tide. "Les was in his early teens, when his mother drowned. I suppose it had its effects on him. They say he was close to her. And that he has never really forgiven Captain for taking her out against her will. A psychiatrist could make something of it. The way Les goes out of his way to flaunt convention, for instance." He shook his head. "I didn't bring you here to brief you on the Lenhart family tree," he said. "Is it warm enough to walk?"

"I have this." She lifted the collar of her wooly sweater.

"Let's do, then. Okay?"

She nodded, wishing that she hadn't worn heels, thinking that the sand would be warm. She could kick them off; tuck them under her arm . . .

They followed the curve of the harbor, to where it joined the headland. Surprisingly enough, there was a stretch of beach, invisible from above, along the base of the overhanging cliffs.

"There's something I want to show you," Dr. Catrell said. "If it doesn't get dark too soon. I don't think it will, if we hurry. Dusk lingers a long time, here." He slipped his arm through hers, and noticed that she was struggling, in the heels. "I'm sorry," he said, at once. "I didn't think . . . "

"It's quite all right." She stooped to slip the red shoes off of her slim feet, the sea breeze, gentle this night, wrapping the soft folds of her skirt around her knees.

"Your hose . . . "

"I'll slip them off, too," she said, not making an issue of it, but sliding her hand up beneath her skirt to unfasten garters. She turned modestly to slide the cobwebby stockings down slender legs, accepting his offer, as a leaning post. "There. I've always loved to run barefoot in sand." She squirmed her toes, hoping that he didn't think her too childish, and telling herself that every foot-weary nurse should have an equal opportunity to ease away her tiredness.

It was exciting, walking beside the tall, dark-haired doctor, feeling the give and pull of the sand, warm beneath her naked feet. They came to a log, washed by high tide onto the beach. Dr. Catrell released her hand, and sat down on it to remove his own shoes, and roll up his trouser legs.

"I can't let you have all of the fun,"

he grinned at her, setting their shoes side by side on the log. The rolled up trousers gave him a long legged, little boy look. His legs were brown, Holly noticed, as though he swam on sunny days.

He reached for her hand again, and she gave it to him, liking the warm clasp of his fingers around her palm, wondering where he was taking her, asking, in the next instant, above the sudden fluttering of her heart.

"My secret hideaway," he told her, his square mouth stretching in a wide grin. "The Lenhart mansion is above us, on the headland. If you'll look closely, you can see the tips of the spruce that grow around the motel, just above those rocks." He pointed, and Holly picked out black shapes against the graying sky. "I've carved some stairs in the face of the headland, back of the motel. They're too precarious, still, for general use. I plan to install wooden steps, and a railing. When I do, we can step out our back doors, and come down to the beach whenever we please. That is, if a patient doesn't call."

They laughed together, in complete understanding.

The beach was narrow, with black rocks jutting just offshore. The sea swirled savagely around them, creating a frantic undertow. Yet, brave people did swim in the cold, coastal waters. Dr. Catrell, Holly suspected, was one of them. He spoke as though he expected her to stay at the Headland Motel for some time. And it pleased her. San Francisco and Brian seemed a million miles away, here on this seawashed stretch of Oregon sand. The crash of the foam-capped waves seemed to wash all thought of him from her mind.

The keening sea birds, startled from rocky perches by their approach, added tenor notes to the bass drumming of the breakers. They were below the motel, now. The beach was wider here, secluded by monstrous dark rocks. The high tide swirled around their bases, eddying to form small, receding pools in their lee. The yawning mouth of a cave appeared suddenly, in the base of the cliff, partially concealed by rocks.

"This is it." Dr. Catrell pulled her toward the yawning black opening, with a gentle tug of his hand. "I didn't know about this cave, when I bought the motel from Captain Lenhart. I doubt if he did. Few people bother to follow the beach along the cliffs, with all of that sand around the harbor mouth."

"There's something eerie about it," Holly said. Almost as though on cue, a shadowy form appeared in the vague, dark cave mouth. Holly gasped.

"It's only a man." Dr. Catrell's husky voice reached to reassure her. "A few old beachcombers know about this place. They're harmless."

She let him lead her toward the dark figure that moved toward them, in the falling darkness, separating itself from the dense blackness of the cave. It had grown too dark to make out features clearly.

"Hello!" Dr. Catrell called.

"Who are ye and what are ye about?"' The reply was hardly more than a croak, mingling with the cries of the startled gulls.

Holly concentrated her blue gaze on the dark shape, and made out the form of a man huddled in a black slicker. The startling contour of a pegleg protruded below the voluminous garment.

"Pegleg Tom!" she gasped, relief surging through her.

"Good girl!" Dr. Catrell said. "Tom!" he called. "It's Dr. Catrell." He released her hand to hurry toward the old man. "Don't you know you're trespassing, you old reprobate." His deep voice competed with the sea, winning out over the battering crash of waves, as he greeted the old man with a happy shake of his gnarled hand, and a hearty slap on the stooped shoulders.

He was genuinely glad to see the

ancient saw sharpener, Holly thought, coming up to them. She acknowledged the introduction Dr. Catrell was making, impulsively reaching out a small hand, letting the old man grasp it in rough, fishy fingers.

"You're early, Tom," Dr. Catrell said. "I didn't expect you to hit Ocean Breeze for another two weeks."

"I've got me a real job cut out," Pegleg Tom said. "A smart man like you maybe already knows this, Doc. But I'll tell ye anyway. It's the year for another big tidal wave. Happens every fifty-year, regular as clockwork."

Holly shivered, remembering the premonition she had felt, the night she and Dr. Catrell went to the Howe place to pick up Margaret. The old man's words sounded ominous. Her blue gaze sought Dr. Catrell's face, that had become no more than a blur in the falling darkness. He sensed her fear, and reached for her hand, squeezing it a little.

"What has that got to do with this

job you mentioned?" he asked, seeming unimpressed by the old man's dire prediction.

"I've took it on myself to warn folks," Pegleg Tom said. "I've got this whole coast to cover. I seen one of them big waves wash this coast clean fifty year ago. I don't want to see nothing like that again."

"It gives Pegleg something to do. Makes him feel important," Dr. Catrell told Holly, when they left the old saw sharpener alone at the cave, to start back down the beach. "Some of the local businessmen are glad to hand him a bottle of wine, through a back door, to get rid of him. If he can pass along a startling piece of news in the process, he no doubt feels he's earned his coveted drink. It's easier than sharpening saws."

"But, if a tidal wave should come, it could destroy Ocean Breeze, couldn't it?" Holly asked, thinking how near the water the town lay, not to mention Jinx Jones's scrap yard, across the harbor.

The old mill site had been flooded, once. It could happen again.

"The water would back up the river, for some distance," Dr. Catrell said. "No doubt the folks who built this town took that into consideration. There have been some minor swells. Some homes have been flooded. But there's never been any really serious damage."

"There was something scarey about running onto that old man," Holly said. "Will he be warm enough, in the cave?"

"He'll build himself a driftwood fire if he's not," Dr. Catrell said. "Pegleg Tom can take care of himself. He didn't have to choose that way of life. So we can assume that he enjoys it."

"He's so old," Holly said. The excitement she had felt, when they started along the beach, had fled, leaving her suddenly tired. And a little chilled . . . She walked close beside the tall doctor, grateful for the sheltering warmth of his big body, between herself and the hungry sea.

"Don't let that queer old man's tales frighten you away," he said. "I need you too much to let that happen."

"A nurse doesn't frighten easily," Holly told him. "I'm not going away. Not for awhile," she added, remembering Brian. Dr. Merdahl was counting on her to come back to him. And when she did . . .

She felt on her finger for the diamond ring he had given her, and remembered that she had left it behind in San Francisco. "For safe keeping," she had told her parents. Although that hadn't been her only reason for slipping the sparkling bauble from her finger, and tucking it safely into the family safe deposit box. She wished again, seeing the questioning expression in Dr. Catrell's eyes, as he opened the pickup door for her, and helped her inside, that she had worn it to Ocean Breeze.

"I hope not for a long while," he said quietly, climbing in beside her, starting the throbbing engine.

"So do I," she heard herself saying.

8

THE sun was shining brightly when Holly awoke the following morning. She slid slim legs over the edge of the bed, and hurried to the windows, to let streamers of sunlight flow into the cozy rooms. Beyond the rim of the headland, the Pacific looked subdued and innocent, its sparkling surface reflecting a dozen pure shades of blue.

She was humming, when she slid up to the counter in the little cafe.

"You look bright and shining this morning," Gen Byrde said, almost resentfully. "Your date with Key last night must have been a success."

"I wasn't aware that it was a date," Holly said, pulling the morning paper toward her.

"It will be taken for one in this town," Gen's voice was strained. She stooped to take a can of syrup from beneath the counter, not looking at Holly.

Gen *cared* about Dr. Catrell, Holly thought. And why not, she told herself, in the next breath. He was a handsome man. Virile. Desirable. It wouldn't be difficult to fall in love with a man like Key Catrell. Especially when a woman saw him every day. Cooked his meals. Cleaned his office. Or worked beside him in his office . . . The idea pleased and frightened her at one and the same time. She snipped if off with precise, mental scissors.

Gen was a pretty woman. Voluptuous in a suggestive way. The kind of woman men noticed, Holly categorized her. Although she hadn't noticed that Dr. Catrell paid any particular attention to Gen. But there had been that moment, the night before, when Gen had jokingly warned Holly against Dr. Catrell, and the man at the counter had hinted that Gen knew what she was talking about . . .

125

"Dr. Catrell wanted to acquaint me with your town, since I'm going to be living here," she told the bright-haired woman, longing, unexpectedly, for the hard, cold feel of Brian's ring on her finger. There would be no need to explain, then. She searched for words to tell Gen that she was spoken for.

"I noticed that you had your shoes and stockings off, when you got back," Gen said, before she could speak. "You must have gone to the beach."

"Now that's a scandalous thing to do." The cafe door jingled closed, behind Holly. She turned to see Les Lenhart behind her. "There's only one reason to go to the beach here," he added, sliding onto the stool beside her, never taking his blue-white eyes from her face. "You being a stranger in town, you might not know what it is. Want me to tell you?" The bright eyes dared her.

"Leave her alone, Les," Gen said, unexpectedly.

"Someone has to wise her up on

the local customs," Les said. "I'd hate for her to get stranded down there on the beach with the wrong guy, not knowing."

"Les!" Gen snapped. Some intangible current seemed to flow between the two.

"You afraid Catrell will take me on, and get hurt?" Les asked, his voice harsh. "Or is it just that you've got a dirty mind? Anyone but you would know that the reason we go to the beach, in Ocean Breeze, is to hunt seashells." The burly chest, each roped muscle detailed beneath a thin, white T shirt, expanded in a great guffaw of cruel laughter.

As suddenly as it had exploded into uninhibited mirth, his almost boyish voice grew serious. He turned to Holly. "I didn't come here to poke fun at Gen," he said. "Actually, I thought I might be lucky enough to see you. Maybe even have breakfast with you. That is, if you don't mind."

The change in his character was

startling. Unexpected. The glowing, blue-white eyes became subdued, as though he had pulled some invisible screen across their shining iris, closing off some inner fire. He could have been any ordinary, blond young man, handsome, polite, a little shy, even, asking a favor of her.

"I don't mind," she heard herself saying, feeling glad that she had, when he glanced suddenly at Gen, his face apologetic, to tell her he was sorry.

"I've heard that before" Gen snapped. But her face softened, beneath his charm, as she turned to set steaming plates of hotcakes before them, rich with pools of butter.

"I'll walk you to the office," Les Lenhart said, when they finished.

"It's only . . . " she started to protest, then looked up to see the mirth in his strange eyes. They laughed together. She found herself attracted, in an uncomfortable way, to this man with the Mr. America build, and fiery eyes.

"This place belonged to me, you

know," Les commented, when they stepped outside. "Captain wanted to set me up in business. But I was a bad little boy, so he took it away from me, and gave me the old mill site as my share of the Lenhart enterprises. I suppose he figured it would wash away sooner or later, and I'd be left with nothing but a bare patch of sand," he flashed bright eyes at her. "I fooled the whole town. Made a success of that mess of driftwood that was left after the mill flooded, and Captain rebuilt upriver. Jinx Jones is the man in charge," he added, seeing the questioning look in Hollys' blue eyes. "Most people think he owns the wrecking yard. But I'm the man behind the man. He makes good money for us both. That way, I don't have to work. Just sit back on my yacht, and collect my share of the earnings."

The man *was* slightly mad, Holly mused. They had reached the door to Dr. Catrell's office. Les reached past her to open it, his thick, hard arm brushing her own.

"I must get to work," she told him, drawing away to step inside.

He stuck his head through the doorway, to glance around the plain, beige and brown waiting room. "Still the same old place," he said. "I'm well off rid of it. I wasn't cut out to be a motel man."

"I find it quite comfortable," Holly told him, wishing he would go. The first of the day's patients was due.

"So does Gen," Les said. "She'd give anything to get her hands on the deed. She was saving to buy this place, when Captain sold it to Dr. Catrell." He shrugged mammoth shoulders. "Now there are rumors that Gen is out to trap Doc, just to get her hands on this dump. Security. That's what a woman like Gen is after."

"I really do have to get busy, now," Holly told him, without comment.

"I'll vamoose, and let you get to your pills and plasters after you've answered a question for me," he said. "That is, provided you give me the correct answer." His blue-white eyes sparked. "Would you do me the honor of going yachting with me this weekend, Miss Doran? The weather man says it's going to be fair, and the harbor master has promised me clear sailing."

"I . . . " He had caught her completely off guard. She sucked in a deep breath to steady herself. She did have to get busy, and he had promised to go, if she said yes. There could be no harm in spending an hour or two on the water, with him. "Yes. Why not," she heard herself saying.

She let out her breath in a long, deep sigh, after he had gone. "What have you gotten yourself into now, Holly Doran?" she asked herself, half-aloud, wondering what Brian would say, if he were here.

But he *wasn't*. And she was glad, she told herself, going to her desk, in the small, glassed-off cubicle that separated her station from the rest of Dr. Catrell's cozy waiting room.

She glanced at the appointment book, and forgot about Les Lenhart, as she began preparation for the patient who was due any minute. A vasectomy, scheduled for nine — a young man from the mill who had more children, now, than he could afford, if all of the youngsters, whose cards were filed with his, belonged to him. She laid the record card on Dr. Catrell's broad, masculine desk, and hurried into the small surgery to prepare for the minor operation.

The day progressed swiftly. Seeing the little stack of cards on Dr. Catrell's desk, when the last morning patient had gone, Holly realized what an astounding number of people had passed through the office that morning. And another surge of patients was due at one. She had better hurry . . . She swept up the stack of record cards, with a small, but efficient hand, and tucked them carefully back into the file. She didn't realize that Dr. Catrell had come into the room, until she heard his voice behind her.

"They're all falling in love with you," he said. "Every single patient. Not that I blame them any." His square mouth spread in an appealing grin. "It's good to have you here, Holly." His storm-gray eyes met hers, their depths illuminated. Revealing. She read sincerity in them. And something else. Something that made her heart pound with a sudden, wild rhythm. "How about lunch." His voice broke the spell.

"In a second, Doctor." She turned back to the file, feeling color flame through her cheeks, warming their smooth crests.

Men had looked at her that way before. Brian. And, as recently as this morning, Les Lenhart. She had responded to his physical magnetism, to a degree. But never had she experienced a spontaneous response, such as the tall, handsome, Ocean Breeze doctor, standing behind her, had aroused in her with a single, unguarded glance. There had been no little area of reserve, remaining calmly and coolly collected inside of her, as there had been with Les. And, she admitted to herself, with Brian. She felt suddenly vulnerable.

She struggled for composure, tucking the last card into the file, assuming her best professional stance; her most nurse-like smile, as she turned back to him.

"Ready, Doctor," she said brightly.

He tucked his hand through her arm. His touch felt warm and comfortable, through the starched stuff of her uniform. She breathed a sigh, glad that the wild surge of emotion had passed. She would send for her ring, she thought. She knew instinctively that Dr. Key Catrell was the kind of man who wouldn't look at a woman the way he had just looked at her, if he knew that woman was promised.

She knew just as surely that the ring wouldn't have made a difference to Les Lenhart. He would have asked her to go yachting with him, regardless. And Brian had encouraged her to date other men, if an opportunity arose. He would feel that same way, after marriage, she suspected. He was in the habit of taking certain of his female patients to lunch, or dining and dancing, if it seemed that an evening of his brilliant company might help them overcome some personal problem or inhibition. Felicia Onstott, for instance. A woman like Felicia demanded a great deal of her psychiatrist's time. If she went back to Brian, she would have to resign herself . . .

She glanced up at the tall man beside her, his crisp hair shining in the sunlight, glad for his steady presence, thinking that Dr. Catrell would have a different concept of marriage. It was written in the honest, clean lines of his face. A face she had grown to like very much, Holly realized, stifling a sudden — and frightening — impulse to reach out slim fingers and touch the smoothly shaven angle of his firm jaw.

She drew a deep breath, trying to concentrate on Brian, at the same time, making a mental note to write and ask her mother to mail his ring. Perhaps she would be more sensible with it on her finger, as a constant reminder.

★ ★ ★

The next few days were busy ones in Dr. Catrell's small office. There was a rash of accidents, at the mill. A man was struck in the head by a rocketing two by four. Dr. Catrell had suspected a concussion. They had taken the patient to Seal Beach General for observation. Another employee had fallen into the green chain. His hand had been badly mangled, but Dr. Catrell and Dr. Spencer had pieced muscles and tendons together, so that he might have the use of it again. Holly had ridden the ambulance with Dr. Catrell, and scrubbed to work beside him, in the green-tiled surgery, on that one.

It was late Saturday afternoon, and

the last patient had left. Dr. Catrell was washing his hands in the basin. "That does it, for today," he said, when he had finished. "Unless, of course, someone decides to slip, down at the mill, at the last minute."

They laughed, suddenly, together, knowing that if there was an accident, they would be called upon to care for the victim, whether they were still at the office, or not. And they would do it gladly, eager to make the best use of their carefully acquired medical skills. Holly put the thought into words.

"It has to be that way," Dr. Catrell agreed. "But it isn't always easy for a doctor to drop everything, and run, when that persistent telephone jangles. Especially, if he happens to be on a date with a pretty girl. Which is exactly where I intend to be tonight," he added.

Holly felt her thoracic region tighten. Gen, she thought. The red-haired, cafe operator had a girl come in to help her on Saturdays and Sundays. She would be free to go out . . .

"I'll be here," Holly said, trying not to analyze the constriction in her chest, telling herself that it was none of her concern whom Dr. Catrell chose to date. She had her own date with Les Lenhart to worry about.

"Not if I can help it," Dr. Catrell was saying. His words penetrated her mind, suddenly. Her Tahoe blue eyes sought his handsome, tan face questioningly. "You happen to be the pretty girl I had in mind," he stated. "How about dinner in Seal Beach, tonight? Gen's a good cook. But a man likes to plan something gala for his first real date with a girl. Champagne. Live music. Does it appeal to you?"

"It does," she admitted, catching her breath, thinking, with a small, private smile that she was well on the way to becoming the belle of Ocean Breeze, with two different men asking her for a date, her first weekend.

She wondered what Dr. Brian Merdahl would say to that! No doubt, he would assume that she was taking his professional advice seriously, by not letting any one man become a habit, while on her pilgrimage in search of her true self!

9

SHE laid out the daring red cocktail dress, for her date with Dr. Key Catrell. Red set off her dark hair, and brought out the natural color in her high, smooth cheeks. The dress was one of the few things Brian hadn't helped her choose. She had seen it in the window of one of the clever little shops on Maiden Lane, one day, while on her way home from the hairdressers. She had hesitated about trying it on — the dress was one of the new styles, with a low dipping back, defying a modest, high rising, front bodice.

But once on, the dress had pleased her. So much that she had saved it for a special occasion. "Like tonight," she said, half aloud. Thank goodness, she had nice shoulders, she thought, catching a glimpse of herself in the mirror, as she slipped out of her uniform. Two minutes in the shower, and she emerged refreshed, her satiny body glowing. She toweled herself, and stopped to brush her long, dark hair, letting the blood rush to her head, stimulating her scalp. Precisely one hundred strokes, and she tossed the glistening mass back across her shoulders to study herself in the mirror.

The French roll was pert and neat for the office. But for a special occasion, to go with the red dress . . . ? A swinging pony tail, she decided, daringly, made sophisticated by a knot of hair pulled close to her scalp. Deftly, she manipulated the silken mass, with clever hands, achieving the result she wanted, stepping back, and tossing her head a little, to be certain it was just right. It was, she decided, reaching for filmy undies.

The dress, next, its chiffon-over-satin folds slipped carefully over her head, smoothed across her firm, rounded breasts, and zippered snugly around a waist that a big man could span with his two hands . . . She felt gay in the chiffon creation. Gay because she had a date with Dr. Catrell, she realized, growing still, her blue eyes gazing back at her from the mirror, suddenly serious. She had taken great pains to dress for him, she admitted to herself. There had been no such urge to be gay and daring for Brian . . .

Dr. Catrell's tap on the door startled her. She snatched up the flowing chiffon stole that went with the dress, and threw open the door. He stood, not moving, looking at her.

"Holly?" His storm-colored eyes glowed warmly with admiration. He towered over her, breathtakingly handsome in a white dinner jacket, and slim, dark trousers, topped by a cumberbund that emphasized the low, narrow leanness of his waist, and his slimly tapered hips. His crisp hair shone in the evening light.

"Ready, Doctor," she said, feeling

rewarded for her careful efforts. Feeling, too, that the evening was going to be a success.

"You've changed," he said, quite simply. They walked side by side, to his old truck. "Les Lenhart's M.G. might be more appropriate tonight," he added, opening the door for her, helping her in. "But this will have to do."

"This is fine." she said, waiting for him to go around the rattly vehicle, wondering if he had heard gossip about her date with Les. Or had he mentioned the M.G. only because it was red, and would match her dress? For some inexplicable reason, she found herself not wanting him to know about her impulsive acceptance of Les' invitation to go yachting. She had a feeling that Dr. Key Catrell wouldn't quite approve.

The old truck throbbed into action, and they pulled onto Highway 101. The scent of azaleas hung heavily on the air. No vacancy signs had blossomed suddenly at the new motels at the edge of town. Colorful banners, heralding the coming festival, had been strung at intervals above Ocean Breeze's main street.

"This must be an exciting time for Margaret Howe," Holly remarked, a smile lighting her pretty face. "By the way, how was Pete's leg, when you made your rounds this morning?"

"Healing nicely. He'll be able to watch the parade — from a chair, of course. And I've given him permission to wobble around town on a pair of crutches next Sunday. That's the big day, for everyone. They'll crown Margaret officially, and she and princesses will hold court in the azalea gardens." He glanced at her, his gray eyes suddenly bright. "Say, you haven't been up there yet, have you? The azaleas are quite a sight, this time of year. You'll have to see it to believe it," he added. "How about tomorrow afternoon? That is, if something unexpected doesn't turn up at the office."

"I'm sorry, Doctor," she told him, looking into his steady, gray eyes, wishing she hadn't been so impulsive when Les Lenhart asked her to go out on his yacht with him. "I have a date."

"Anyone I know?" he asked, his voice casual.

"Les." It came out almost a whisper. She cleared her throat. "Les Lenhart."

"Oh," he grunted. "Well, some other time for the azaleas, then."

"I'd like that," she said. She had a feeling, as they rattled along the coast, past fields of sword-leafed lilies, that her gay evening had somehow been spoiled.

It had grown dark by the time they reached Seal Beach. Dr. Catrell pulled the pickup into the parking lot of a swank looking club. Glittering signboards, under a striped marquee, boasted live music. A blonde singer. Heads turned, as they entered. She felt Dr. Catrell's warm, firm hand on her elbow, and looked up to see pride in his eyes, as the hostess showed them to their table. Perhaps her mention of Les hadn't spoiled the evening, after all, she thought, letting him seat her, telling herself, in the next breath, that it had been conceited of her to think that it might.

They ordered steaks, thick, rare, juicy, drowned in mushroom sauce. They chatted, over the delicious dinner, their conversation turning naturally to medical topics.

"I'm pressuring Captain to set up a regular clinic. Or a small hospital," Dr. Catrell said. "We'll bring in a couple of good nurses. A technician or two. Another M.D. And a dentist. We'll need new equipment, of course."

"Promise me one thing, Doctor," Holly flashed blue eyes across the table, at him.

"Make it Key, and I will," he grinned at her, his square, mouth looking hard and sure and attractive, in the candlelight.

"All right, Key," she smiled. "Build

your new little hospital on the headland, away from the harbor."

"I plan to," he said. "Primordial instincts, or not. You still have Pegleg Tom's warning on your mind, haven't you?" he added, his husky voice softening, his gray eyes understanding.

"I've thought about it," she admitted. "He seemed like a spooky old warlock, or something."

"He's less ominous, by daylight," Dr. Catrell said. "I imagine he's given up the idea of warning folks, by now. I haven't seen him around. Not since the night at the cave."

"Could it be that he passed along his tidal wave warning, and hurried on to the next town?"

"Someone would have mentioned it. His annual appearance usually elicits a few comments. A piece in the local paper."

"Would he stay there in the cave? An old man like that . . . "

"He's always been healthy," Dr. Catrell guessed her thought. "At any rate, he shuns doctors like they were the plague." His gray eyes took on a worried cast, their storm-colored depths darkening. "I wonder . . . "

"Surely, someone would have found him, if he's ill," she said, remembering, in the next instant, what Dr. Catrell had said, about no one using the lonesome stretch of beach below the headland. "It's been almost a week."

"I know," Dr. Catrell said. "I'll see what I can find out about that old coot, when we get back to Ocean Breeze, just to alleviate both of our minds. Someone will have noticed him, if he left." He glanced across the table at her. "Now, how about taking advantage of that good music."

The four piece dance band had assembled, the blonde songstress taking a turn at the drums, before she stepped up to the microphone to sing. "I'd love to," Holly said, not quite able to put Pegleg Tom out of her mind. If that pathetic old man *was* lying sick, in that cold, damp, sea cave . . .

"You're the most beautiful woman here," Dr. Catrell murmured in her ear. "I'm the envy of every male in the place."

She smiled up at him, putting Pegleg Tom from her mind, becoming acutely aware of the tweedy, masculine scent of Dr. Key Catrell's skin and clothes; of the warm, hard-soft pressure of his hand, against her bare shoulders; his fingers mingling with the silken length of her hair. He would be marvelous to make a habit of, she found herself thinking. To fall in love with . . . If she weren't already in love. And she did love Brian, she told herself. Enough to have accepted his ring. But not enough to have accepted *him* fully, some small, inner voice prompted her thinking.

She silenced the mysterious, inner voice. Conscience, she thought, wondering what Brian would say, if she told him that she had one. Brian, she feared, didn't set much store by conscience. Unexpectedly, she found her thoughts turning once more to Pegleg Tom. It was her nurse's conscience speaking this time.

"Enjoying yourself?" Dr. Catrell's pleasant breath brushed her cheek.

She nodded, the ponytail bobbing against her bare back and his bare hand. "You dance well. It's a pleasure for a woman to find herself in the arms of a man who handles himself well on the dance floor. Just as a nurse enjoys working with a skillful doctor."

"Still the bright, young lady in white, in spite of the red dress," he grinned.

"I'm afraid so." she said. "I was thinking about Pegleg"

"If you had said Les, I'd have been jealous," he said. She looked up into his gray eyes, and saw, with a little, pang that she identified as fright, that he was dead serious.

"I . . ."

"I know," he cut her off. "You can forget I said that. I was thinking about Tom myself. Wondering what's happened to him."

"Maybe we should . . ."

"I think so," he said, before she could finish. "I'll fetch your wrap." He left her at the edge of the floor, near the door, weaving his way, with long strides, among the dancers, to retrieve her chiffon stole. "We'll take up where we left off, another time," he told her, when they had stepped out into the sea-misted night.

* * *

They found the old saw sharpener in the cave.

Pegleg Tom lay doubled up on a pile of rags, near the entrance. A small pile of driftwood smoldered near him, illuminating his huddled body with angry, red light. Several empty wine bottles, and the oiled wrapper from a box of saltines, lay nearby. Dr. Catrell knelt beside the old man, his spatulate fingers gently exploring, even before he spoke.

"What is it, Tom? What's happened here?" He dipped into the black bag, beside him, and brought out a pencil-fine light, deceptively strong, directing the probing ray into the old man's pupils. "He's not drunk," he murmured to Holly, who had squatted beside him, trim in the dark capris she had slipped into, in lieu of the filmy red dress.

The man on the ground groaned, his gnarled hands clutching at his lower abdomen. Dr. Catrell immediately directed his attention to that area of the patient's anatomy, unbuckling the soiled trousers, palpating the pelvic cavity.

"His bladder's like a balloon," he said, seconds later. "When did you last void? Make water?" he added, in response to the uncomprehending look in the old saw sharpener's eyes.

Tom's head rocked back and forth. "It's painin' me so I can't remember, Doc," he muttered. "For God's sake, can't ye do something afore I bust?"

"I intend to, Tom. But not here in this sand. We have to get you to the office."

"We'll need a stretcher," Holly said. "I'll go for one," she added, sounding braver in the darkness than she felt.

"There's no time for that." Dr. Catrell crouched beside the old man, knees flexed, and slid his arms under the aged body. Slowly, carefully, he lifted him, his long back straight, and as strong as steel, Holly thought, acutely aware of his resolute, male virility.

His long legs ate up the black sand with amazing swiftness. She had to run a little, to keep pace with him. She brushed against his shoulder, and felt the corded muscles. Not the bulging, overdeveloped biceps that Les Lenhart displayed, but long, lean, smooth muscles, bearing the old man's weight like bands of steel. She thrilled to the feel of that hard, capable flesh, even as her mind flashed ahead to the office, making quick, mental preparations.

The old saw sharpener managed to make his own way into the office, balancing against Dr. Catrell's steady arm, emitting gasps of pain, with each step.

Minutes later, the old man's pain had been relieved. "Temporarily," Dr. Catrell told him. "It's too late to make an extensive examination tonight. And I doubt if you're up to it. But I may as well tell you, now. I suspect an enlarged prostate. It's common in men your age."

"Ye ain't plannin' to cut, are ye?" Pegleg's round, brown eyes glared from beds of saggy flesh. "I won't have the knife. Can't afford it. Don't want it. I've got work to do, warnin' folks."

"You wouldn't want a repeat of what you've been through tonight. This whole week, if I'm not mistaken. I haven't seen you out and around." Dr. Catrell tried to reason with the stubborn old transient.

"Had a little too much wine," Tom said. "Cut down on my wine, and take a few shots of sea water, and I'll make out."

"I'll fix you up in one of the units

here, for tonight, Tom," Dr. Catrell said. "We'll talk about this again, in the morning."

"I got no money for motel units," Tom said.

"It's on the house, Tom," Dr. Catrell told him.

Holly had finished straightening the office, by the time Dr. Catrell returned from seeing Pegleg Tom to one of the units. She handed him the card she had typed, with Tom written at the top.

"I didn't know his last name," she said.

"Come to think of it, neither do I," Dr. Catrell told her, taking the record card from her, writing down details, his broad hand gripping the pen high on its barrel.

"If that's all, Doctor, I'll leave you now," Holly said. She glanced at her watch. It was one o'clock. Les Lenhart was picking her up at eight.

He laid a restraining hand on her arm, his fingers closing on her firm, warm flesh. She was reminded suddenly of his strength, as he had lifted Tom from the pile of rags in the cave. "I liked the red dress," he said. "Will you wear it for me another time?"

She nodded, a torrent racing suddenly along her veins. She knew he was going to kiss her, even before his long, strong arms reached for her. And she wanted him to, she thought, for all of Brian's glittering diamond, and cautious warnings. His arms closed around her, and his lips met hers, gentle, in their firm demand.

He released her, and held her away from him, his lucid, gray eyes studying her face. "Take care tomorrow, Holly," he said. "I . . . " He bit back what he had been going to add, and turned his attention abruptly back to the record card.

"I will, Key," she told him, feeling a sudden guilt. She should have told him about Brian, long before this. But there hadn't seemed to be an opportunity . . . or a reason.

Her heart was beating wildly, when

she let herself into her own comfortable motel unit. She had lost all desire to go out with Les Lenhart. His invitation had sounded like fun, at the time. Now, suddenly, she found herself dreading it. She would much rather remain at the motel, and assist Dr. Catrell with his examination of the old saw sharpener.

She enjoyed being with Key Catrell, she admitted to herself, regardless of what they might be doing. In the office. On the beach. At lunch, in Gen Byrde's small cafe. She liked his neat, clean, attractive appearance; the way his gray eyes changed from stormy shades to a clear lucidness, that revealed a caring soul. She liked the warmth of his husky voice; and the gentle, hard feel of his mouth, pressed against her own.

She liked him too much, she told herself, thinking that perhaps it was just as well that she was going yachting with Les Lenhart, no matter how much she would prefer to remain behind.

10

THE M.G. pulled to a stop in front of her doorway promptly at eight o'clock the following morning.

"Ready, nurse?" Les Lenhart stuck his grinning face inside, when she called to him, in reply to his loud knock.

"I think so." She tried to sound enthusiastic. "Will I need a jacket?"

"That, and a swim suit," Les said.

"Surely, you don't expect me to dive in with the sharks." She smiled, in an attempt to be gay.

"I know a safe place," he told her.

She went to the closet, for her wooly sweater, and a straw bag containing her red swim suit. "All set," she said, following him out the door, the bag dangling from a slim hand.

"Have you seen Tom this morning,

Holly?" She turned to see Dr. Catrell emerging from the unit he had assigned to the old saw sharpener, his gray eyes concerned. "He's not in his room," he explained.

"Old Pegleg?" Les laughed. "I saw him on the way over here. He flagged me down, in fact. Spouted some weird nonsense about a big tidal wave coming."

Gen Byrde stuck her head out the rear door of the cafe. "I gave him a cup of coffee this morning, before he left," she said. "What was wrong with him, anyhow?"

"Personal," Dr. Catrell muttered. "Did he say where he was going?"

Gen shook her head. "I had the radio on, when he came in. Something on the news set him off. He mentioned something about a tidal wave coming to wash the town away, and lit out. I know he drinks. But I didn't smell anything on him."

"I heard the morning news, on the way over," Les said. "There wasn't anything about a tidal wave. A couple of little quakes up in the Aleutians, or somewhere. Nothing big enough to set off a chain reaction."

"Pegleg no doubt thought they were," Dr. Catrell said.

"Is he sick, Key?" Gen asked, coming to stand beside him.

"He's an old man," Dr. Catrell said. "I expect he'll be back."

"That old coot's not worth this fuss," Les told Holly, putting the M.G. into gear, sending them shooting out onto, the highway, in a burst of noisy speed.

Holly was acutely aware of Dr. Catrell's tall, handsome presence, beside Gen Byrde, watching them go. She was still thinking about him, when she climbed aboard Les Lenhart's trim, white-painted yacht, that glittered with bright-work. A colorful burgee fluttered in the breeze, above the trim, varnished deck. The San Francisco Yacht Club burgee! Holly recognized it at once, her blue eyes questioning.

"I don't spend *all* of my time in

these backwaters." Les seated her on one of the swivel chairs in the cockpit. "Matter of fact, I took a little run down to Frisco a couple of days ago. Karl's wife wanted to go down."

"Louise?"

"You've met her, then?" He started the boat's engine, and clambered to unwind the line from the cleat, agile, for all of his thick muscled brawniness.

Holly watched him, her mind occupied with Louise, wondering if the pregnant woman had returned to Ocean Breeze with Les, and whether or not she would appear at Dr. Catrell's office the following day. It was dangerous for her to go chasing across the waves, in a bobbing boat.

"Why the long look?" Les asked her, as he backed the glistening craft away from the dock, into the mainstream of the harbor.

"I was thinking about Louise," she said. "She shouldn't have been out on the sea, in her condition."

"I tried to talk her out of it," Les

said, good naturedly. "It was a waste of breath. One of her friends down there wrote and told her about a psychiatrist everyone who is anyone is raving about. A Dr. Merder. Or Merdahl. Something like that."

Holly couldn't stifle the gasp that arose in her throat. "Dr. Brian Merdahl?" she asked.

"That's the one. You know him?"

Holly nodded. "He's my fiance," she said.

Les glanced up sharply. "Did I hear right?"

She nodded again, feeling rather foolish, wishing that she hadn't told him. Wishing, too, that she hadn't been so cautious about her ring.

"It's a small world," Les grinned, his blue-white eyes bright with amusement. "You could have fooled me. I assumed you were unattached."

"You don't mind?" She hadn't come out on his yacht in search of romance.

"Not everyone in this hick town is a square." Les laughed, his strange eyes flashing. There was something diabolical about that laugh, Holly thought. "Doc might mind, if he knew," Les added. "But not me. I'm as liberal as they come." He glanced at her. "Say, you must be quite a gal, engaged to a headshrinker. Uninhibited. All of the things the well adjusted female is supposed to be." He laughed the wicked laugh again.

Sudden fear darted through her. "About Louise," she changed the subject, drawing away from his bulging shoulder. "Did she come back with you?"

"She's still down there," Les said. "She wanted to get in a few sessions with your Dr. Merdy, or whatever his name is. She's got some crazy idea about having the wrong attitude toward the baby. It's understandable, I suppose, considering the way she looks. And Karl can't be with her much. He spends his time at the mill. When he's not there, he's off somewhere chasing down buyers. Karl's

the ambitious Lenhart. Me . . . ?"
He grinned at her. "I'm the black
sheep of the family. Don't say I didn't
warn you."

The glimmering white craft bounced
over the waves, leaving the harbor, with
its crouching town, out of sight beyond
the roll and tumble of the white capped
sea. Off to the right, the dark bulk of
the headland arose, stiff against the
softer contours of the coast range.

"There!" Les pointed suddenly. She
turned her head, and saw a small, blue
inlet, glowing like a jewel between high,
sand-colored cliffs, not more than a
half mile above Dr. Catrell's cove.
"My own private cove," he grinned,
turning the helm, guiding the small
yacht expertly between the towering
headland. A stretch of yellow-gray
beach came into view, circumventing
a perfect circle of inviting, blue-green
water, illuminated by dancing sunrays.
No wonder Margaret Howe was crazy
about Les, Holly thought, if he was in
the habit of bringing his dates to this

delightful little paradise!

"You can change below, in the cabin," he told her. "I'll drop the pick, and ferry the lunch basket ashore. I had Gen fix a little something," he added, seeing her look of surprise.

She hadn't intended to stay away from the motel all day. A case might come in . . . And there were her uniforms to launder; the winged, white caps to be starched . . .

She put the thought into words.

"You don't take a yacht out for fifteen minutes," Les told her, irritation tinging his voice. "A sophisticated girl like you should know that."

Apprehension sliced through her. She went into the small, but elaborately appointed cabin, wishing, again, that she hadn't come, longing suddenly, for the comforting sound of Dr. Catrell's reassuring voice. She slid the brass bolt on the cabin door, not trusting the fiery-eyed man outside.

She had to admit, later, that it was pleasant swimming in the sun-warmed cove. The blinding sun rays beat down on her skin, turning the droplets of water on her arms and legs to salt crust, when she lay down on her towel to get warm. Les chose to do brief exercises, his magnificent body gleaming. She had been wrong not to trust him, she decided. So far, he seemed to take a greater interest in himself than anything around him.

"I believe in keeping fit," he told her, seeing her blue eyes on him, flexing an arm to mountainous proportions, for her to admire.

She closed her eyes, not speaking.

And felt, suddenly, his mammoth strength pushing close to her. Her blue eyes flew open, to see his face bending close to hers. "My physique didn't seem to impress you. Maybe a little kiss will," he said, his lips drawing back to bare white, perfect teeth that were, Holly realized crazily, quite false.

She sat up, her hands thrusting out against him. She knew it was hopeless, even as her flying hands came into contact with his hard, muscle-bound body.

"Impressed?" He drew back from her, his hands still on her shoulders.

She was too frightened to speak.

"I suppose a girl like you has dated some of the best of them." His strange eyes glowed. "But even you will have to admit you don't see a body like mine, often." His great chest bowed out, puffing with some twisted pride. And I'll lay you ten to one, I can kiss better than the best of them."

"You're sick," she managed, aware of a harsh, popping sound above the crash of waves, outside the mouth of the tiny inlet. Seconds later, she realized what it was. The sound of a boat's motor! She tried to call out. But no sound came. She sucked in her breath, willing her strong, firm nurse's discipline to come to her rescue, reminding herself that she had been trained to cope with every type of patient. Deliberately she thought of Les Lenhart as the disturbed man he was.

"You . . . do have a beautiful build, Les." She groped for the right words. "I'll have to . . . admit that I've never seen . . . such muscles, before." Somewhere, in the back of her mind, she heard the sound of the boat growing nearer. If she could keep the huge, blond man beside her, occupied with flattery, until whoever was in that boat came to within screaming distance . . . "You must have plenty of girls crazy about you," she rattled on. "A man with your looks."

He leaned toward her again, his mouth determined, closing in on her own. A shadow fell across her. She raised her blue eyes to see Dr. Catrell standing, like a miracle, behind Les Lenhart, water dripping from his crisp hair, his blue denims clinging to him like a skin. He whipped out a steel-banded arm, and clasped his fingers, grown suddenly vise-like, on Les Lenhart's shoulder. With one terrible, flinging movement, he pulled the brawny man away from her. In the next instant, his fist cracked against flesh, and Les staggered backward.

"Are you all right, Holly?" He knelt beside her. Les, regaining his balance, loomed behind him.

"Key!" Someone screamed. She realized it was herself. And screamed again.

The two men grappled on the sand, one broad and round muscled, the other lean, with long, steel-banded arms.

"No sense . . . wearing yourself out over her, Doc," Les managed to blurt. "She's . . . engaged. She belongs . . . to a headshrinker . . . named Merdahl."

Dr. Catrell seemed not to have heard. Holly watched the two of them roll in the sand, a terrible, sick, helpless feeling surging through her. Blood began to drip from Key Catrell's nose, staining his square mouth, the handsome chin. Dr. Catrell pulled free of Les's grip. She saw, with a weak flow of relief, that Les was tired, when he lunged at Key Catrell, missed, and fell panting.

He rose again, and turned on Dr. Catrell, rushing forward, his bull-like shoulders poised for the tall doctor's abdomen. Dr. Catrell sidestepped him, his long arms lashing out with cable-like strength, to clip Les Lenhart beneath the jaw. Slowly, in strange, langorous motions, Les Lenhart crumpled to the sand.

Holly rushed to him, kneeling, her nurse's instincts alerted.

"I didn't hurt him," Dr. Catrell said. "He'll be all right." He regarded her coldly, his storm gray-eyes unfathomable. A droplet of blood dripped from his chin, to trickle down his chest.

She arose, wanting to go to him, to press his bruised face against her breast. He turned from her, a distant look shielding his eyes. He *had* heard Les, then, she thought, unspeakable pain slicing suddenly through her heart. In that precise instant, Holly Doran knew that she had fallen in love with the tall, headland doctor.

11

D R. CATRELL didn't mention his fight with Les Lenhart, when she entered his cubbyhole office the following morning. He shuffled through the stack of cards, when she laid them on his desk, not looking at her. "Where is Louise Lenhart's card?" he asked, seeing that it was missing.

"She won't be in today," Holly told him. "Les took her to San Francisco. She's seeing a psychiatrist there."

"Did Les mention his name?"

Holly felt her cheeks grow warm. "Yes. As a matter of fact, he did. It's . . . Merdahl. Dr. Brian Merdahl."

He glanced up sharply, his gray eyes bright. "Isn't that the man . . . "

"Yes," she said, before he could finish, thinking that it would have been much better if she had been the

171

one to tell Dr. Catrell.

"Les had some idea that your being an engaged girl justified his ungentlemanly actions yesterday," he said.

She had the uncanny feeling that he had been able to read her thoughts. "Brian . . . Dr. Merdahl and I . . . had some difficulty, before I left San Francisco," she managed. "That was my reason for coming here. I needed to get away."

"You returned his ring?" The gray eyes flashed to her left hand.

"Not exactly. We hadn't decided on anything final. I needed time away from Brian, to . . . to find out some things about myself." She found herself wanting to explain.

"I see." His gray eyes were non-committal. "Would you get me Louise's card, please?"

She went to the file, feeling that she had made a terrible mess of things, realizing, as her fingers flipped through the tightly packed cards, that she wanted Dr. Catrell's respect, as a woman, as well as in her capacity as a capable nurse, more than anything she had ever wanted before in her life. And his love . . .

She didn't know who he was calling, until she heard his rich, husky voice speaking into the mouthpiece of the telephone. "Is Dr. Brian Merdahl there, please?"

Her heart caught in her throat. Shamelessly, she lingered outside the door of his small, cramped office, trying to hear.

"I believe you are treating a patient of mine, Doctor. Louise Lenhart. Yes. That's right."

She drew a deep breath, and hurried down the corridor, to show in the first patient, not waiting to hear the rest. Brian would be speaking now, telling Dr. Catrell about Louise in that half-bored, sophisticated way he had. She was glad she couldn't hear.

The morning passed quickly. And, just as she and Dr. Catrell were leaving the office to go to Gen's for lunch, Pegleg Tom came, stumping along on his greasy wooden leg, his leathery skin creased.

"Now don't ye go getting that light in your eye, Doc, like ye was plannin' to take out your knife and use it on me," he croaked. "I'm fine, I am, since ye relieved that bit of pressure. A little too much of the bottle is all it was. I come back to weed your flowers for ye, for the use of the bed. Could have got me a job in town, but no point fixin' up things what are doomed to wash away."

"When is this tidal wave due, Tom?" Dr. Catrell asked, his face entirely serious.

"Any day, now. Any day," Tom said. "I feel it in my bones."

"He's dead serious, isn't he," Holly said, when they were seated inside the cafe, over Gen's special for the day.

"Tom doesn't quite know how to be any other way," Dr. Catrell said.

"There could be something in what

he says," Gen commented, leaning to place brimming cups of coffee beside each plate. "According to the news, they're still having some shakeups in the Aleutians. One big one, and that old Pacific out there could go berserk."

"Tom's turning Gen into a doom monger, like himself," a man at the end of the counter laughed. "I hate to see that happen, Gen. You've always been fun."

"Oh, go on with you, Hank." Gen turned her saucy back on him.

Dr. Catrell ignored the exchange, turning his attention on Holly. "People don't have time to worry too much about Tom's warning, with the Azalea festival coming up," he said. "They're too busy making plans for next weekend. How about you?" he added. "Have you made yours?"

She shook her head.

"Good," he said. "I'd like to squire you around to all of the important events, if you'll let me."

"I can't think of anyone I'd rather

have for an escort," she smiled, intending to sound bright and flirty, hearing, instead, her voice uttering words weighted with meaning. And, in the next instant, seeing a subtle change come into Dr. Catrell's eyes.

He had forgiven, her, she thought, for not telling him about Brian. She felt as though a weight had been lifted from her trim, white-clad shoulders!

★ ★ ★

Ocean Breeze teemed with activity, when they drove down off of the headland, into the main street of the small town. Almost overnight, it had been transformed from a drab, salt-encrusted hamlet into a blossoming tourist mecca, its motels filled to capacity, the trailer parks along the river lined with elaborate homes-on-wheels.

Dr. Catrell swerved the pickup, shifting gears to gain momentum for the climb up from the river, to the bluffs where the azaleas grew. Moments later, they emerged into a world of pink and salmon and orange flowers.

Holly caught her breath, sucking in the heady, almost musky, scent that saturated the air, rich as honey. "I've never seen anything like it," she said. "They're beautiful."

"Ocean Breeze's pride and joy, these gardens." Dr. Catrell stopped the truck in a graveled parking lot, beside a small, red sports car. An M.G. She turned questioning eyes on him, as he helped her from the high vehicle.

"Les's," Dr. Catrell said.

"He didn't strike me as the flower-loving type," Holly said, letting him lead her along a flowery path.

"I doubt if Les's interest in coming here is horticultural," Dr. Catrell said. "Most likely, he has a rendezvous with one of his girlfriends. These gardens are used frequently for that purpose." Then, seeing the warm glow that spread across Holly's smooth cheeks, "I'm sorry, Holly. I'd forgotten . . . "

She managed an embarrassed little laugh. "I made a fool of myself by going out with Les Lenhart," she said. "It takes awhile for a girl to forgive herself a mistake like that."

"At least you can smile about it," Dr. Catrell reached out a warm hand to pat her arm. "If Les had meant something, you might not have managed that."

"He was just someone to go out with," she blurted, wishing after it was said that she had remained silent.

"And me?" he asked, his rich voice coming from deep in his chest. "Do I fall into that same category?"

There was no escaping the silent demand in his gray eyes. She groped for words, thinking of Brian, and wishing that she had broken off with him completely before coming to Ocean Breeze. How was a girl to find herself, she wondered, unless she were free to follow the dictates of a heart gone suddenly wild inside her rib cage? Without warning, his strong arms reached to enfold her. A fleeting thought whipped through her mind, as his hard, square mouth found hers. She had *wanted* him to kiss her again, she realized, in that gentle, painfully sweet way . . . The little edge of fear she had felt, when Brian forced her to yield to his demanding, almost savage embrace, was gone. She let the tall, crisp-haired doctor press her into the curve of his hard body, his firm mouth banishing all thought of Brian.

He released her, one arm cradling her shoulders — shoulders that trembled with a rare, surging excitement.

"That makes a man wish you were free." His gray eyes, grown lucid in the half-light, searched her own. His broad hand found hers, to lead her in silence, through the great, sprawling gardens.

They were unaware of the shadowy figures embracing beneath a towering spruce, until they were almost upon them. A huge, muscled blond man, and a tawny-haired girl. Les Lenhart, and Margaret Howe! The two separated with a guilty start.

"For Pete's sake, Doc. Do you have to come sneaking around everytime I romance a girl?" Les blurted, his blue-white eyes bright in the semi-darkness.

Holly felt Dr. Catrell's hand tighten on her own. The lean, handsome face above her remained calm.

"We're looking forward to seeing you crowned tomorrow, Margaret," he said, ignoring Les, not pausing in his long legged stride, as he and Holly passed beyond the startled couple.

"We came to pick my bouquet for tomorrow," Margaret gushed behind them. "The queen always carries azaleas."

"She shouldn't be here with him," Holly said, when they were out of earshot. "Les is so much older. And . . . "

"I know," Dr. Catrell said. "But we can't interfere."

"Ethics," Holly said, knowing that a person must ask a doctor, first, for help. And neither Margaret, or Les, had asked.

She was still worried about the girl, when they arrived back at the motel, an hour later. She didn't notice the shiny black, torpedo-shaped car, parked in front of Gen Byrde's Headland Cafe, until Dr. Catrell pointed it out to her.

"Gen's drawing the carriage trade tonight," he remarked. "Quite a contrast between that swank buggy, and Pegleg Tom's mode of travel," he grinned.

Holly glanced at the car. And looked again, her blue eyes widening with surprise. Long, low, chrome-appointed and custom built — she had seen only one other like it, in all of San Francisco. And that particular one belonged to Dr. Brian Merdahl. It couldn't be . . .

She glanced through the windows of the small cafe, and saw the tall form of a man. A slim woman was seated beside him.

It *was* Brian! And Felicia! One slim hand flew to her mouth, to stifle a gasp.

12

"**D**ARLING!" Brian slid off of the counter stool, his long arms reaching, his dark eyes smoldering at the sight of her slim, capri-clad body; her amazed blue eyes.

"Spare us the dramatics, please, Brian dear." Felicia's throaty voice floated across Brian's suave shoulder. The psychiatrist ignored her, his face closing in on Holly's.

She turned her head, forcing a little laugh. "Really, Brian! In front of everyone?"

"Bravo, darling!" Felicia Onstott purred, her wide-set green eyes on Holly. "The male animal thwarted. You'll have to wait for your kiss, Brian, dear."

Holly was painfully aware of an audience. Gen, busy at the grill, her jade-colored eyes knowing. And Dr.

Key Catrell . . . She was still keenly aware of the feel of his lips. She hadn't wanted Brian to destroy their azalea sweet flavor.

Dr. Brian Merdahl glanced beyond her, seeing Dr. Catrell, sensing, in the same instant, that he and Holly were together. A faint gleam, that Holly recognized as displeasure, lighted his brown eyes.

"My rival?" he said, the thin line of his mouth smiling below suspicious eyes.

"Dr. Key Catrell," Holly made introductions. The two men shook hands, warily, Brian's dark eyes not missing a detail of Dr. Catrell's casual dress.

"I brought back your patient, Doctor," Brian said. "Louise Lenhart. I talked to her, after your call, and convinced her that she should heed your words of advice. You must have a way about you, Doctor. She refused to see the specialist I recommended. Insisted on coming back here."

"Where is she?" Dr. Catrell asked, ignoring the insinuating look in Dr. Merdahl's eyes, his own eyes mirroring concern.

"We dropped her off at that morgue the Lenharts call home," Dr. Merdahl said. "She was tired, from the drive. I administered a sedative, and advised her husband to put her to bed." He turned abruptly to Holly. "Now that my professional duties have been attended to, let's find a place to talk." He clamped her arm in a firm grip, turning to Felicia. "You don't mind, do you, dear?"

The radio blared suddenly, cutting off the sophisticated woman's reply.

" . . . the worst shakeup yet. The quake lasted less than two minutes, but during that fateful time, entire buildings tumbled," the crisp tones of the announcer's voice held their attention. "It was feared the entire chain of islands might be submerged. Officials can only guess at the number of casualties. Stay tuned to this station for further bulletins."

"Pegleg should be here," Gen said. "Is there any real danger, Key?"

"There could be," Dr. Catrell said. "We'll be alerted, of course."

"What are they talking about, darling?" Felicia Onstott slithered off of her stool, turning to cling to Brian's arm.

Holly shuddered. It couldn't happen, she thought. Not with the town full of tourists. Those trailer houses by the river . . .

"One of our local characters has been predicting a tidal wave," Dr. Catrell was saying. "There's a chance that the water will rise. Maybe innundate the streets along the harbor. But you've nothing to worry about, here on the headland." He glanced at Brian, his gray eyes calm. "We'll need you, Doctor, if an emergency does arise. We haven't enough . . . "

A car, careening into the circle of light cast by the motel sign, cut him short. His tall, lithe body tensed into immediate action, even before

185

the car door flew open, to reveal Terry William's pale, frightened face. Dr. Catrell was out of the cafe door, in two giant strides. Holly followed, shrugging off the long, slender hand Brian reached out to restrain her.

"Something's wrong," she tossed back over her shoulder. "Key needs me."

Key needs me . . . Some remote part of her mind fastened onto the unconsciously uttered words, even as she leaned into the car, beside Dr. Catrell, and saw Pegleg Tom's limp body huddled on the back seat. She couldn't stifle the little cry that arose in her throat, at the sight of the old man's face. It was gone, part of it.

"Dear God," Dr. Catrell murmured, even as his big hands reached to grasp the old man's dangling wrist.

"He's still alive, Doc," Terry Williams said. "I been keeping him alive. But he needs more help than I can give him, no matter what Les and Jinx said."

"What have they got to do with

this?" Dr. Catrell barked.

"Les did it," Terry said. "Pegleg come to the junkyard a couple of days ago, to warn us about a tidal wave. Les thought he was getting nosey. They scuffled, and Les got good and mad. He . . . he threw lye on the old man."

"I didn't believe even Les was capable of a thing like this?" Dr. Catrell said, lifting the old man out of the car. A new car, Holly noted almost unconsciously, as she hurried before him.

There wasn't a great deal they could do for Pegleg Tom. "It's times like this that I pray for a small hospital here," Dr. Catrell said, unwinding gauze bandages from his arms, his big hands gentle, as he examined the gelitanous tissue. "He'll need plastic surgery."

Terry Williams sat in the waiting room, his thin face pale. He should be at home, in bed, Holly thought, and told him so.

"I ain't going anywhere, until I know how Pegleg's going to be," he said. "I should have brought him right after it happened. Only Les wouldn't let me. He said he'd . . . " He cut himself off short. "But never mind that. How is he?

"Not so good." Dr. Catrell appeared in the hallway, behind Holly. "But he could have been worse, if someone hadn't treated him."

"I did, Doc," Terry said. "I read somewhere that boric acid solution was good for a lye burn. I been irrigating those sores on Pegleg every hour, since it happened."

The ambulance came screaming over the brink of the headland before Dr. Catrell could question Terry further. "I'll be back as soon as possible," Dr. Catrell told Holly, climbing in beside the old saw sharpener, when he and Joe Green had finished loading the stretcher.

"I guess I'll be going back to Mom and the kids," Terry said, when the ambulance had gone. "I've had enough of Les Lenhart, I don't care how much of a big shot he is."

Holly watched him get into the new car, and drive off, noticing, before she turned to go back into the office, that it had a California license plate, thinking, with a little corner of her mind, that maybe Guy Kessler had been right about the stolen car ring. If Les Lenhart could push people into saws and burn them with lye, he was capable of anything. And that would explain how Jinx Jones remained lucrative, in spite of the undiminishing heaps of scrap.

She was so busy with her own thoughts, she didn't see Brian, until she walked into his reaching arms. In the excitement, she had forgotten about him. She wriggled free, feeling suddenly irritated with him for coming.

"I thought you'd never finish with that old bum," he was saying. He guided her toward his low-slung, expensive car. "Get in, darling. I'll drive you to your place, and we can talk."

"This *is* my place," Holly told him.

"You mean . . . ?"

"I live here," she said. "In one of the motel units."

"I might have suspected some such unconventional setup, when I heard that sexy voice over the telephone," Brian said.

"Since when have you been concerned with convention, Brian?" Holly asked, a rare anger burning in her blue eyes.

"That's why I'm here, you know," he continued, as though he hadn't heard her. "I guessed, when your Dr. Catrell called me about his O.B. patient, that he wasn't the harmless old G.P. I had imagined him to be. Then, when you didn't write, I thought it was time to do some investigating. Louise Lenhart gave me a good excuse for coming."

"And Felicia?" Holly heard herself asking, wishing, in the next instant that she hadn't.

"Jealous, sweetheart?" Brian's grin looked diabolical in the colored light cast by the motel sign.

"Where is she?" Holly asked, noticing that Felicia was gone; refusing to dignify his question with an answer. She realized, even as she spoke, that it really didn't matter one way or the other to her where Felicia was.

"At the Lenharts'," Brian said. "We're house guests there. I drove her over there, while you were busy," he added. "I wanted to see you alone. I hope this impetuous little act won't cost me my most lucrative patient. Oh." He grinned the wicked grin. "I almost forgot. Felicia came along as chaperone. Not that Louise needed one, in her bloated condition. Does that answer your question, darling?"

"You should get back to her, Brian," Holly said. "I have things to do."

He reached for her hand — and felt the bareness of her ring finger. "That reminds me." He remained surprisingly unperturbed. "I have a surprise for you."

"It will have to wait until tomorrow,

I'm afraid," Holly told him. She turned to go. His long hand snaked out, and captured her. Twisted her toward him.

"You still haven't kissed me," he said.

"I . . . "

He leaned over her, the thin line of his mouth closing over her own, in a savage kiss, cruel and demanding. She pulled away, and ran toward the brightly lighted office, with its modest shingle and restful waiting room, wondering if Brian knew how to be patient and gentle. Like Dr. Catrell . . . The comparison popped into her mind, against her will. She brushed it aside, and busied herself in the cluttered room, where they had worked together over the old saw sharpener.

13

IT was nearly midnight, when Dr. Catrell returned. Holly, knowing that she couldn't sleep, had remained in the office, rearranging the files, and catching up on correspondence. She had wanted to be there, when he returned, she admitted to herself, her heart quickening at the sound of his husky voice saying goodnight to Joe Green.

"Holly!" He seemed surprised to see her still there when he stepped through the doorway. He glanced at the neat little stack of letters on the corner of her desk. "Those could have waited," he said. "I expected you to spend the evening with your . . . with Dr. Merdahl."

The jangling of the phone saved her from an explanation. Dr. Catrell reached for it, his handsome face patient, his kind voice reassuring. "Dr. Catrell." Then, "Yes. Yes, Pete. We saw her earlier. In the gardens." He paused, his gray eyes dark with concern. "No, she wasn't alone. She was with Les Lenhart. I had an idea you didn't know. Listen, Pete. I'll take a run out there, if it will make you feel better . . . "

"Has something happened to Margaret?" Holly asked, when he hung up.

"She isn't home yet," Dr. Catrell told her, his voice tense. "Pete can't go looking for her, with that leg. I told him I . . . "

"I'm going, too." She blurted the words, remembering the way Les Lenhart had forced his unwanted attentions on her.

"A good idea," Dr. Catrell commented, his gray eyes understanding her unspoken thought. "I have a feeling this is going to be one of those nights. Tom's accident, if you can call it that. And now Margaret . . . It stems from the festival. All of the excitement and high spirits invariably lead to a rash of mishaps."

She hurried along beside him, climbing in on her side of the pickup, thinking that he was right about the accidents. There had been a heavy flow of patients, at Mercy, just before the big holidays. Broken arms. Lacerations. Twisted backs, Bruises. And rapes . . . She let the ugly word creep in, not wanting it to, but considering it, because she was a nurse, involved with the most vulnerable aspects of human behavior.

The Azalea Gardens were deserted, when they arrived, the flower laden bushes seeming suddenly ominous in the dark night. There was no sign of the red car. Or of Les Lenhart and Margaret Howe. Dr. Catrell got out of the truck, and called the girl's name, his voice booming on the night stillness. Holly held her breath, awaiting a response that didn't come.

"The next best place to look is the

harbor," Dr. Catrell said, climbing back into the truck. "Les may have taken her out to the yacht."

They drove in silence, down the slope to the main road along the river, past the mill and the Victorian houses crouched near the dark harbor. The Howe house was the only one still lighted. Dr. Catrell stopped the truck, and they strained their eyes for some sign of the sleek, white craft, that should have been anchored outside the circle light cast by the dingy lamp at the head of the dock. The sound of water, lapping persistently against the rugged timbers of the wharf, licking the scaly hulls of the anchored craft, came to them. There was something sinister about the sound, Holly thought, remembering Pegleg's warnings, and the more recent newscast.

"The yacht's gone," Dr. Catrell was the first to put the new fear into words. "Les should have known better than to take that girl . . . " He bit off the angry words, slamming the pickup into gear, backing out of the parking area, with a spurt of sand. "I'll talk to Pete," he said.

Holly huddled beside him, silent, as they drove back along the street, and came to a screeching halt in front of the Howe residence.

"Come in," Pete Howe called, before Dr. Catrell could press the doorbell. "Did you find her?" Pete hobbled toward them, when Dr. Catrell pushed open the door.

"Sorry, Pete." Dr. Catrell said. "I have an idea they've gone out on Les's yacht. She's not at anchor."

"I'll have Les thrown in jail for this," Pete said.

"Do you want me to call the Coast Guard?" Dr. Catrell asked, his voice calm.

"It's the only thing. I don't know what possessed Margaret to do a thing like this." Pete Howe hobbled into the kitchen. Holly heard him dialing, then hanging up the phone, without having spoken. He came back into the room, his face sagging; his eyes bright with worry. "I can't do that," he said. "If I call the Coast Guard, the paper will get ahold of it, and spread it all over the front page of tomorrow's special edition. There'd be a scandal."

"We'll go." Dr. Catrell glanced at Holly. Her blue eyes met his, willingly. Confidently. "I have an idea where those two might be."

We'll go . . . He had included her as naturally as though she had always been a part of his scheme of things. The thought sent sudden warmth through her veins, driving out the fear she felt.

Outside, she gradually became aware of a difference in the sound of the sea, beyond the broad mouth of the harbor. And in the hungry lapping against pier and boat and shore. She stopped beside the parked truck to listen.

"I hear it, too," Dr. Catrell said, beside her. He reached out to put a strong, warm arm around her shoulders.

It was a rising, swelling sound, as though the entire sea were moving. Lifting. "A tidal wave?" The question escaped her soft lips on a frightened gush of breath.

"A swell," Dr. Catrell said. He helped her into the truck with steady hands. "The town will be all right, so long as it doesn't get any larger." He pointed in darkness, toward the harbor shore. "There's leeway for quite a spill-over. More than you'd imagine."

Holly shivered a little, as they drove onto the street that fronted the harbor. She became suddenly aware of the greasy expanse of swollen water, beyond the salt-dimmed glow of the street lamps, and saw that the beach was no longer visible, across the street from Pete Howe's house! The oily, dark water had crept to cover it.

"Key!" She reached to lay a soft palm on his hard arm, letting his strong, male warmth reassure her.

"Don't be afraid, Holly," he said. "The water's beginning to recede. We'll take Pete up to the motel, just to be on the safe side. The Coast Guard will warn the local authorities. If there's any real danger, they'll let people know in time."

"What about Margaret?" Holly asked. "And Les . . . "

"I have an idea Les took her to the cove. They'll be safe, if he has sense enough to take the yacht out, when he discovers these swells. It's a graceful craft. It will ride the crest like a gull," Dr. Catrell said. "I think we'd best not try to look for the girl. I'll explain to Pete. These waves may be the reason Les hasn't come in sooner. I hope they don't get any larger," he added. "Pegleg's prediction could come true."

She longed suddenly for the security of the headland and Dr. Catrell's small, efficient office. And for the safety of the tall, gray-eyed doctor's arms . . . She severed the thought with a firm, mental scalpel, watching him stretch long legs out of the pickup, and hurry toward

Pete Howe's front door. She had no right to think about Dr. Catrell, in those terms. She forced her thoughts to turn to Brian, as she waited for Key Catrell to emerge from the house with Pete Howe.

There was no comfort in the idea that she belonged to Dr. Brian Merdahl. No security. Brian would love her savagely, and selfishly, taking from her to fill his own erratic needs, that she knew. But would he be there, his arms strong and willing, when *she* needed comfort? Most likely he would stand back and analyze her little fears, she thought, a small smile curling her lips at the idea. It was so like Brian . . . She *could* smile about it, in spite of her uneasiness. It came to her that she was doing a bit of analyzing herself. And it was about time, she conceded. After all, she had come to Ocean Breeze to discover some things about herself, and that should include an evaluation of her own personal needs.

The two men came to get into

the truck, Pete Howe's face more concerned than ever. Holly moved to the middle of the narrow seat, to make room for him. She was painfully aware of the hard, warm pressure of Dr. Catrell's lean body against hers, as he slid beneath the wheel. She had developed a very definite need, she thought, as the old pickup rattled to life. One that only a tall, strong, gentle man could fulfill. A man like Dr. Key Catrell.

14

ALTHOUGH it was well past midnight, a light was on at the motel, when they arrived with Pete Howe. "Key!" Gen Byrde came out to meet them. "Captain's been trying to reach you since midnight. It's Louise," she added. "Convulsions, Captain said."

"Dear God." Dr. Catrell breathed the words in the form of a prayer. "Make Pete Howe comfortable, Gen," he ordered. "And prepare all of the units. There are some swells rolling in down on the harbor. They could get worse."

Gen nodded. "They've been putting out warnings over the radio. And the State Police called."

Dr. Catrell turned to Holly. "We'll need drugs. Supplies."

She nodded her dark head, already

running down the corridor. It took her mere seconds to slip into the fresh, crisp uniform she kept hanging in the supply room. Eclampsia. Her mind formed the thought with dread. *If medical management of the convulsion should fail to bring about an improvement in the patient's condition, labor must be induced.* The information flitted through her mind, leaving a residue of fear in its wake. If they had to deliver Louise, in that eerie, old mansion . . . Thank goodness Brian was there, she thought again, going to the small surgery for forceps, wrapping them carefully in sterile towel, as she began preparation of an O.B. bag.

"Ready, nurse?" Dr. Catrell came to take the bundle from her, his black bag swinging from one big hand, and a bundle that Holly knew contained the precious intravenous equipment already tucked under his lean arm.

"Ready, Doctor," she said, her mind flitting in a last minute tabulation. Satisfied that she hadn't forgotten anything, she climbed into the truck beside him, for the drive across the headland.

For the first time, since she had come to Ocean Breeze, lights blazed from every window of the Lenhart mansion. Captain Lenhart met them at the door, his darting eyes bright with worry.

"Karl was called out of town, this afternoon, on business," he said. "I couldn't reach him. Louise is in the room at the head of the stairs," he added, urging them along. "That psychiatrist fellow from San Francisco is with her. Said he knew what had to be done, until you got here."

Louise Lenhart writhed on a ponderous bed, set in the middle of a large, mahogany paneled room. Brian bent over her, suave, even at a moment like this, in a maroon-colored smoking jacket, his dark face remote. Distaste. Holly analyzed the expression in his dark eyes.

"She's in the delirium stage," he

said, his voice as remote as his face.

Dr. Catrell took his place beside the bed. "Quiet, now, Louise," he said softly, reaching with a broad, comforting hand, to restrain the distorted body from falling off of the bed, as she bowed her back, in pointless, physical activity.

Holly dipped into the black bag, for morphine and scopolamine, noting that Brian had put a gag on Louise's mouth, to keep her from biting her tongue. Seeing, too, that Louise's face and hands were puffed to frightening proportions. Her B.P.R. would be even more frightening, Holly couldn't help thinking. The pregnant woman must have lived on salty foods and sweets, since she had visited Dr. Catrell, in spite of his warning.

"I'll be outside, Doctor," Brian turned, not offering to stay, and left the room.

She helped Dr. Catrell administer the Stogonoff treatment, forgetting the sophisticated psychiatrist during the next few moments, as they worked together over the patient. They must keep her from slipping into a coma, Holly thought, hurrying from the room to prepare saline for catharsis in the bathroom two doors down the hallway.

Brian emerged to block her path, reminding her once more of his persistent presence. "Still the dedicated girl in white," he said, glancing at the enamel basin she carried. "I . . . " One of the numerous doors opened, and Captain Lenhart emerged, interrupting him.

"She's still the same," Holly answered the unspoken question in the little man's birdlike eyes.

"I think Key should get her to Seal Beach," Captain said. "While there's still time."

"We can't move her, as she is," Holly told him. "When her present condition has improved . . . "

"It may be too late, then. The night watchman at the mill just called to tell me that there have been several big swells. The State Police are warning people down along the harbor to evacuate. If a big wave does move in now, the bridge will go."

Holly felt Brian grow suddenly tense, beside her. "That means I won't be able to get back to San Francisco," he said.

"Why not, darling?" Felicia Onstott appeared, seductive in flowing marquisette. "What's happened?" She looked at their concerned faces. "Don't tell me that hideous old man's prediction has come true."

"Not yet, Felly," Brian said, laying a slender hand on her arm. "But there's a chance it will. I think it's time we vacated this mausoleum." He glanced at Holly. "The three of us," he said, pointedly.

"You can't be serious!" Holly said, shock showing in her blue eyes. "I couldn't leave Key . . . Dr. Catrell, now. Even if I wanted to," she added, her soft lips set in a firm line. "Nor should you, Brian. He may need both of us."

"He'll manage, darling," Brian said. "He did, before you or I came. There's no reason why he can't resume his independent ways, after we've gone. It was my intention to take you back with me, when I offered to bring Louise home. Otherwise, I wouldn't have come."

"Don't forget that I am an R.N. On duty," she added emphatically, starting down the corridor with her container of warm saline. Brian followed, reaching to restrain her, with an insistent hand. The other hand slipped into the satin-lined pocket of his smoking jacket. He drew out a bright bauble, and held it toward her, his dark eyes glowing.

"The surprise I mentioned last night," he said.

It was a diamond. Her diamond. The one she had accepted from Brian, when he asked her to marry him. It seemed like eons ago. As though it had happened to another girl, far removed from herself.

"Where did you . . . ?"

"Your mother told me you had left it behind. And why," Brian told her. "When I called to tell her I was coming to see you, she thought I should bring it. She's a bit prudish, I'm afraid. It didn't seem proper to her that her engaged daughter should be running around loose up here, with a bare finger." A crooked grin creased one of his dark cheeks. He reached for her soft hand. She drew away from him.

"Not now, Brian," she said. "Dr. Catrell is waiting."

"You don't really want to wear my ring, do you, Holly?" he said, his dark eyes glinting with a sudden penetrating light.

"Brian, this is neither the time, nor the place."

"I believe it is," he said. "Since I will be leaving in a few moments, with, or without you. The decision is yours to make." His voice took on harsh, ominous tones.

"I can't leave Dr. Catrell," Holly stated firmly. "Not now." Or ever. The thought drifted out from the remote recesses of her mind. She gave voice to it, her softly spoken words hardly more than a whisper. "I won't wear your ring again, Brian," she added, wishing that she might have found a more tactful way to tell him.

"So that's the way it is," he said, his voice hard. "You've decided to become a permanent member of Catrell's harem. I might have guessed, when you explained your domestic arrangements to me. Living there at that motel . . . I'll have to admit, Holly, that you are prettier than the red-headed one."

Gen Byrde! Brian thought that she, and Gen Byrde . . . A sick feeling surged through her at the knowing look in his eyes.

"I'm sorry you think . . . what you do, Brian," she said, her blue eyes unflinching beneath his burning gaze.

"How could I think otherwise," he stated. "It's an innate trait of all males, human or otherwise, to collect as many females as possible. I'm well aware of that tendency, as a psychiatrist. And as a man," he added, a wicked light burning in his eyes. "Nor is your Dr. Catrell any exception. And you, my dear, like the redhead, are wholly female."

"I have work to do." She refused to acknowledge his deductions.

"Don't tell me she is actually turning you down, darling," Felicia Onstott drawled, coming to cling to Brian's arm. Her green eyes lighted on the glittering ring he held between sensual fingers. "You hardly seem the type to resort to that measure," she added. "You wouldn't have been happy."

15

HOLLY hurried off down the corridor, thinking that Felicia Onstott was right. She had never really *liked* Brian, she admitted to herself, as she pushed open the door to Louise Lenhart's room. She had been infatuated with him. Had even thought herself to be in love with him. But liking was quite something else again. Brian would never be happy with one woman. He had the same as admitted that.

She hurried up to the tall doctor bent over the struggling woman in the bed, realizing that she was lucky to have discovered the truth about Brian before it was too late. And about herself. She wanted a man who had respect for himself. And for others. A man like Dr. Catrell. The storm-colored eyes regarding the puffy face of the pregnant woman were warm with compassion and a true regard for human life. A man's respect for himself reflected itself in his attitudes towards others, Holly thought, setting the container of saline on the bedside table, and preparing to administer the cathartic that would help to eliminate the toxins from Louise Lenhart's swollen body.

They worked together, in silence, administering the glucose, laving the sick woman's stomach, administering oxygen, from the small, hand tank.

An hour later, the convulsions miraculously ceased.

"I believe we're going to be all right, now," Dr. Catrell said. "We'll get one of the boys to bring the ambulance up from the mill. Get her to Seal Beach and induce labor. It's an extreme measure. But one that may save this girl's life."

"You can't do that, Key." Captain Lenhart came into the room, his eyes bright with excitement. "I've just had word that a big swell took out the

214

bridge and half of the town. The police have asked me to open the house to survivors."

Survivors! That meant that there had been a loss of life. There would be injured to care for, in addition to Louise. They would need Brian, Holly thought. He had neglected the skills acquired during the required years spent in medical school. But he could splint a broken arm. Bandage lacerations. If only he and Felicia hadn't gone . . .

"Dr. Merdahl and Miss Onstott left shortly after you talked to them," Captain Lenhart told her. "Merdahl said he couldn't take a chance on being stranded here, with his own patients to attend to."

"We'll manage without him," Dr. Catrell said, his gray eyes meeting her blue ones. "Thanks for staying, until this is all over, Holly," he added. Then, before she could open her mouth to explain. "I had an idea why Merdahl was here, when I saw the way he looked at you," he said. He turned away from her. "We'll begin pit drip stimulation." The order, tossed over his shoulder was firm.

"Can I help, Key?" Captain Lenhart asked.

"I want you to improvise an incubator for your grandchild, Captain," Dr. Catrell told him. "A large box, lined with warm blankets. An electric blanket, or heating pad, will help. I'll improvise oxygen, with a capsule tank."

The baby would be premature. Frighteningly so, Holly thought, taking green soap from the O.B. bundle, telling herself that they would be fortunate if they saved both mother and child. Louise Lenhart lay upon the bed, exhausted, dozing from the barbiturates they had administered. They'd have to use ether. Not much, but enough to induce nausea. She would clean the emesis basin, after she had prepped the patient.

Holly worked quietly. Efficiently. She was only half-aware of the sound of cars pulling into the driveway outside the roomy old mansion.

"More patients," Dr. Catrell said, flashing a reassuring smile across Louise Lenhart's distorted body.

"We're going to be busy here for some time. I'll step outside and see what I can do for those they're bringing in, while you prep the patient."

She raised blue eyes from the area she was smearing with green soap, to watch his tall, straight back disappear through the doorway, realizing that she could have traced every angle and line of that back, and of his tanned, handsome face, without having glanced up.

He was back, by the time she finished shaving the pubic area, his gray eyes relieved.

"There's nothing serious so far," he said. "Thanks to Pegleg, most of the folks along the harbor have been on the alert. Captain is putting some of the families with small children up here." He bent over the patient, his gray eyes alert for signs of recurring convulsion.

"We're still okay," he said, his arm inadvertently brushing her own. His gray eyes caught and held hers. "I hope you won't be sorry you came to work for me, after this night is through," he said. "I need you."

I need you, too, she wanted to say. A long, drawn out wail escaped Louise Lenharts lips, before she could form the words.

"Now we're starting to get somewhere," Dr. Catrell said. "This should be over with quickly." He reached for the sterile, surgical gloves Holly had packed in the O.B. bag.

"Doctor wants to examine you," Holly told the patient, gently urging her to lie crossways on the big bed, arranging her pitifully swollen body in a dorsal recumbent position, and deftly draping her with a sheet placed over the upper portion of the body. She folded a second sheet over the lower portion of the patient's trunk, before turning back the soft, expensive gown she wore.

"Will . . . the baby . . . live," Louise asked, seeming to realize, for the first time, what was about to take place. "Karl . . . will never forgive me, if it . . . doesn't. I won't forgive myself."

Brian had done Louise some good, Holly thought, except that it was too late. A six and a half month baby wouldn't be easy to save, especially if it showed signs of toxemia. She sliced through the negative thought, moving to assist Dr. Catrell.

There was time, when he finished the examination, to slip into the hallway for a much needed cup of coffee, brought to them, by Captain Lenhart.

"Mrs. Green has taken over my kitchen," he explained. "She's getting some hot food into those half-drowned folks down there." Holly recognized the name of the man who drove the mill ambulance.

"How are things in town?" Dr. Catrell asked.

"Several blocks flooded. Buildings damaged," Captain Lenhart said. "To tell you the truth, I'm worried about Les. He left early last night. Said he might take the yacht out. He's stayed away all night, before. But this night has been different. I had the Coast Guard try to get in touch with him, by radio," he added. "There was no response."

Margaret Howe, Holly thought. She had forgotten about Les and Margaret, in her concern for Louise Lenhart. She glanced at Dr. Catrell, knowing by the worried look in his eyes that his thoughts, too, had returned to the absent pair.

"Les had a girl with him," Dr. Catrell told Captain. "Pete Howe's daughter. Pete's over at my place, half out of his mind."

"I'm sorry," Captain said. "Les never could resist a pretty face. But I thought he had sense enough to stick to women like Gen Byrde."

Dr. Catrell's expression changed almost imperceptibly, at his mention of the redhaired woman. "That's over and done with, Captain," he said.

"Sorry again, Key," the little man said. "I suppose she deserves a chance to make something of herself, the same as anybody. And Les, too. I've been hard on him. Now that he might be in danger, I find that I care, for all of his shiftless ways."

"I've known that all along, Captain," Key Catrell said. "I hope, for your sake, and for Pete's, that those two show up, or at least get word to us, soon.

"When Les is out with a girl, he doesn't pay attention to anything else," Captain said. "If this thing caught them in that cove . . . " He ended the sentence on an ominous silence.

A cry from Louise's room sent both Holly and Dr. Catrell hurrying back through the open doorway.

16

LOUISE LENHART'S son made his entry into the world at dawn. Miraculously, the tiny, wriggling mite gasped for breath, expanded his small, wet lungs, and squawled. Holly almost cried with joy. "He's breathing!" she told Dr. Catrell. "He's going to be all right."

The busy doctor had delivered the child, and handed him immediately to her, while he attended Louise. "He seems surprisingly well developed," he said, his own face lighting up. "It wouldn't surprise me to discover that Louise had her dates mixed up."

Nor did the baby show any signs of toxemia! Luck was with them, Holly decided, hoping that it was with Les and Margaret, as well. All night, and still no word from them . . . There had been two more giant swells, during the early morning hours, according to reports from the little town, below the headland. The more seriously injured had been brought to the mansion on the headland. And, somehow, she and Dr. Catrell had managed to care for them, between Louise Lenhart's pains. Captain Lenhart had volunteered to stay with Louise, while they bandaged lacerations, and splinted broken bones.

Now that the delivery was over, and Louise no longer exhibited a frightening tendency toward convulsions, they could tuck the perfectly formed infant into the warm bed Captain had prepared for him, and check on the patients who occupied every spare bed in the big house.

If only Brian had stayed, Holly thought, assisting Dr. Catrell with a woman who had received a bad foot injury. But he hadn't . . . He and Felicia Onstott had run like frightened rabbits, at the first hint of disaster. No doubt, they were halfway to San Francisco, by now. And, if it weren't for the fact that Brian might have assisted them, she wouldn't care, Holly admitted to herself.

"We'll do what we can here, and get over to the motel," Dr. Catrell said. "I'll ask Mrs. Green to stay with Louise. Thank goodness there are enough able bodied women here to look after these people, until other arrangements can be made."

"There's no hurry about getting them out of the house, Key." Captain Lenhart stepped into the room, in time to catch the doctor's words. "Nobody uses these rooms." He paused. "There's still no word," he said.

"Send someone to the motel, if I'm needed," Dr. Catrell said.

"I'll do that," Captain Lenhart told him, his small, bird-like eyes still bright in his leathery face, in spite of the fact that he had been up all night.

They hurried out the front door of the big house, into surprisingly bright, and innocent, sunlight, and all but bumped into Guy Kessler.

"Is Les here?" he asked, his face grim.

Dr. Catrell shook his head. "Didn't anyone tell you? He and Margaret Howe are missing."

"I've been too busy for anyone to tell me anything," Guy Kessler said. "I came to arrest Les."

"What's this, Guy?" Captain Lenhart appeared in the doorway behind them. "Have you got word of Les?"

"I hate to be the one to tell you this, Captain," Guy Kessler said. "But that boy of yours is involved in car stealing. When the big wave receded, it took the old mill buildings with it. There were a dozen new cars inside, all of them stolen. Jinx Jones put the finger on Les, as the brains of the outfit. And seein' as how he owned the old mill . . . "

"He told me he got a share of the profit from the junked cars Jinx sold," Captain said, sounding suddenly old.

"There were a couple of kids involved, too. Terry Williams and some others. They claim Les was in on it all. He

225

even helped load the cars onto that old tub that Jinx claimed was ferrying out his scrap. The kids drove the cars up from San Francisco for them."

"But all of that junk. Jinx bought every wreck for miles around."

"Part of the scheme," Guy Kessler said. "When he got a wreck in, he sent word to Frisco to his highjackers, telling them to pick up one just like it. They transferred the motor number and titles from the wreck to the stolen vehicle, and no one knew the difference. Even took the original paint off of the stolen cars, with lye, so a scratch wouldn't give them away. They waited until Festival time to bring in a big batch, figuring it'd be safer with all of the tourists around. That wave couldn't have come at a worse time for them."

"I . . . I'll call you, Guy, if Les comes in." Captain Lenhart seemed to sag all over.

"Like I said, Captain, I'm sure sorry to be the one to tell you a thing like this," Guy Kessler said.

"What about Terry Williams?" Dr. Catrell asked the round-eyed police officer. "I think that boy could make good, if given half the chance."

"The kid seemed glad to be found out," Guy Kessler admitted. "He's not quite eighteen. I think the law will go easy on him."

"I hope so," Dr. Catrell said. "He didn't have to bring Tom to me. No one would have missed the old coot, until next year." He reached out a long arm to steer Holly toward the truck. "We weren't far from wrong, when we played detective," he said.

"I wish we had been," Holly said.

"I know." His husky voice was rich with understanding.

★ ★ ★

It took them less than five minutes to reach the motel. Gen Byrde greeted them, at the door of the cafe, her green eyes tired; her ripe face devoid of makeup. "All of the units are full," she told them. "I kept the healthy ones here, and sent the injured over to Lenhart's. I thought, with two doctors there, that was best."

"Two doctors?" Dr. Catrell's eyebrows lifted. "Miss Doran's . . . Holly's fiance," Gen explained.

"Dr. Merdahl left for San Francisco last night," Holly said quietly.

"We'll look in on Pete," Dr. Catrell said, without comment. "He must be crazy by now, over Margaret."

"He is," Gen said. "He's been up all night, hobbling around on his crutches. He got in a call to the Coast Guard, before the lines went out. They promised to let him know at once, if they found anything." Surprisingly, her voice threatened to crack. "I keep thinking about Les," she added. "He's really not as bad as everyone makes him out. Sort of like an overgrown schoolboy . . . This thing Guy is accusing him of. It's terrible, I know." Her voice *did* crack.

"I suspect Gen still has a soft spot

for Les," Dr. Catrell told Holly, when they left the small cafe.

"I suppose if you really love someone, you don't get over it easily," Holly said. Then, seeing his gray eyes fill with a question, she knew that he was curious about Brian leaving so abruptly — and did not want to talk about it, just yet. "Do you think there's hope for Les and Margaret?"

"A doctor never stops hoping," he said, his voice meaningful; his eyes saying more than the words. Her heart took up a furious pounding, inside her rib cage, as she hurried after him to check on Pete Howe.

Pete wasn't in his room. They found him on the large, dark rock, behind the motel, looking out over the endless expanse of blue dappled Pacific. The sea looked deceptively innocent, in the benign, morning sunlight. Only the giant, white capped combers, rolling in from as far out as the eye could see, belied the beauty of the restless ocean.

"There's nothing out there, Doc," Pete said. "Nothing but water. You'd think the Coast Guard would have found something by now. If my little girl . . ." He broke off, his eyes looking suddenly old and sunken.

"These things take time, Pete," Dr. Catrell laid a consoling hand on his shoulder. "If Les took the yacht to the cove . . ."

"It ain't that far, Doc," Pete said.

A seagull careened overhead, and swooped again, its shrill cry shattering like china, against the clear, blue sky. Farther out, over the water itself, so that they looked down on them from the headland heights, other gulls were gathering. They had found something in the water. A dead fish, perhaps. Holly watched them, glimpsing a bright fragment bobbing in their midst. Before she could point it out to Dr. Catrell and Pete, it was gone. And visible again, riding the crest of a wave . . . For a brief instant, it rose to flutter feebly against the sky. It appeared to be a burgee! It *was!* Holly caught her breath sharply. The brilliant colored burgee Les Lenhart had flown on his yacht . . .

"Key!" She grasped his arm, pointing. He leaned close to her, his breath grazing her cheek, his gray eyes following the line of her pointing finger.

"Part of the yacht," he said. "With the burgee still attached."

The bright speck of color seemed to be beckoning.

"Where?" Pete Howe bungled onto his crutches. Dr. Catrell snaked out a long arm to keep him from tumbling over the precarious edge of the headland. "Dear God," the big man said, when he sighted the miniature bit of flotsam, as it emerged again from a wave trough. Tears welled unexpectedly in his eyes.

"Come on back to the motel, Pete," Dr. Catrell urged. "We'll get word to the Coast Guard that we've spotted wreckage. The best we can hope for is that Les and Margaret weren't on the yacht, when it went down."

"If they were in that cove, they'd have been trapped." Pete Howe put the fear they all felt into words. "There's no way out, up those cliffs. If only I had my two good legs . . ."

"I've got mine," Dr. Catrell said. "I'll go down there, Pete. I know it won't be easy on you, having to wait. But if Margaret's there, I'll bring her to you." He added words of encouragement. "There are ledges along those cliffs they could have climbed up on. Les has that much sense."

He would need his bag, well stocked, Holly thought, only half-hearing him, dashing off to the office to tuck fresh supplies in the worn, black leather case. And to prepare her own small bag. If Dr. Catrell could make his way down the cliffs, she could, too. There were the crude steps he had carved. Chances were that he would need her, if Les and Margaret *were* down there somewhere on the lonely stretch of beach.

The tidal wave had deposited an abundance of debris and dead sea life on the sand. Holly picked her way through it, avoiding stepping on translucent jellyfish and the broken bits of pearly shell, that shimmered in the sunlight, her blue eyes alert for some sign of Les and Margaret. Dr. Catrell strode ahead of her, leading the way, kicking aside water logged planks — some of them white, like Les' yacht, Holly couldn't help noticing.

They had made their way inch by inch to the beach, clinging to the precarious steps Dr. Catrell had carved into the face of the headland, behind the motel. And had made it safely. Now, if only they could find Les and Margaret. Alive. Holly breathed a little prayer.

"It's not far to the cove," Dr. Catrell said, over his shoulder. "I hope, for Pete's and Captain's sake, and Gen's, that we find them there. Alive." He echoed her thought.

They continued in silence. The beach narrowed, just before they reached the opening in the cliffs that formed the entrance to the cove. Boulders, some of them as large as a small house, blocked their way. Dr. Catrell found footing on them, and climbed upward, reaching down to help her. Little pools of water, left over from the tidal wave, glittered in the hollows and crevices.

Beyond the rocks, the cove came into view, subdued breakers frosting its blue surface. The sketchy little strip of sand emerged from the rocks, to reach around it. Holly looked across to the other side, where she and Les Lenhart had swum, trying not to think about that day, her blue eyes searching.

"There!" Dr. Catrell shouted suddenly, his free arm lashing up to point. "There at the end of the cove, below the rocks."

Holly followed the line of his arm, with her blue gaze. And saw a shape crumpled on the sand, barely out of reach of the waves.

"Oh no!" She stifled the exclamation with a slim hand, willing her firm nurse's discipline to come to her rescue.

Dr. Catrell was running, suddenly, skimming the wet sand, startling little flocks of gulls, come to feed on the dead sea life. Or on bits of food washed ashore from the wreckage. Holly tried not to think beyond that, letting her full reserve of nurse's courage blot out the picture of horror that threatened to flood her mind, thinking that Les Lenhart had been wearing blue, when she and Dr. Catrell saw him in the Azalea Gardens. Margaret had been dressed in pink, the same shade as the musky flowers. Her blue eyes scanned the rim of the little bay, searching for some sign of a girl's pink dress.

There seemed to be only sand, beyond that matted bit of blue.

Les Lenhart was dead. Holly knew, the instant she saw his face. The fire, in the startling blue-white eyes, had been quenched. Dr. Catrell closed them gently. There was no sign of Margaret.

"Do you think you can make it back to the motel, for help?" he asked.

She nodded, aware of an ache somewhere inside. There was always a sense of loss, she thought, no matter how often a nurse witnessed death. The little aching emptiness was always there.

"There may be someone on their way down here, by now," he said. "We'll continue the search for Margaret, after we get Les's body out of here."

It was necessary to do that, Holly knew, because of the gulls. She knew, too, that there wasn't much hope, now, for Margaret Howe. She swallowed the ache in her throat, thinking that she would have to tell Pete what they'd found, as she started back along the base of the cliffs.

She had almost reached the big rocks, when she glanced upward, and saw something pink fluttering against the face of the headland. The same shade of pink as Margaret's dress had been. It *was* a scrap of the girl's dress. She was sure of it, as she put down her bag, and ran to investigate. It had caught on a rock, just out of her reach. The wet line along the face of the sandstone cliffs showed that the tidal wave had swelled to that height, during the night. And higher . . .

Her heart fell. The pink scrap, torn from the girl's dress, meant that her body must have brushed against the rocky headland; that it most probably had been crushed, as Les Lenhart's had.

She wasn't aware that she was crying, until she felt tears hot on her cheeks. She brushed them aside, and turned to, go back and tell Dr. Catrell what she had found, glancing up once more to be certain the pink scrap *was* the same shade as the dress Margaret had worn. She noticed, for the first time, a small ledge, jutting out from the headland, just above the high water line, barely wide enough for a seagull to perch on. Her blue eyes focused on it in sudden horror.

A girl's limp hand dangled lifelessly, over the edge of it, all but obscured by the harsh outcroppings of rock. Some restless, angry quirk of the sea must have deposited Margaret's body there, she thought, crying out, in the next instant, to Dr. Catrell. "Key!" She called again, trying to make herself heard above the roar of the sea, outside the mouth of the cove. She could see him crouched beside Les Lenhart's body, brushing the sand away from the dead man's face, straightening the matted clothes, preparing him as best he could for the party who must come and help him carry the body up the cliff.

He had heard her. And was coming. Running.

She turned back toward the cliff, seeking a way to climb up to the ledge, dreading what she would find there, yet knowing that it must be done.

There were footholes in the sandstone, as though, someone had climbed up before her. And rocks that afforded a grip of sorts. She had managed to pull herself up to face level with the ledge, by the time Dr. Catrell reached her. One more step . . .

It *was* Margaret lying there, the pink dress all but torn from her body, her tawny hair matted, her hazel eyes closed against the horror that had overtaken them. Holly reached out a hand to touch the bruised, young arm. And let out a cry.

She had expected the cold clamminess of death. But the arm she touched was warm and pliant. She noted, with a nurse's automatic instincts, a terrible bruise on one temple, blood caked, and the girl's color was bad. But she was alive! "Alive!" She cried aloud, to the man below her.

His face lighted with some terrible, inner joy, even as he climbed toward her, reaching to help her from the precarious perch, then, drawing

Margaret's limp body to himself, with one strong arm, clinging to rock with the other, as he eased himself down.

He laid the girl on the beach, bending over her at once, to lay his ear against her young breast, using that age old method to determine her condition, in his urgency.

"Thank God," he murmured, his gray eyes bright. "Thank God."

17

MARGARET HOWE was alive. It was Holly's first thought, on waking the following morning. The girl lay sleeping in the bed opposite hers, looking as fragile as a child. A feeling of well-being flooded Holly's heart, and disappeared as suddenly as it had come as she remembered Les Lenhart.

She had gone with Dr. Catrell to tell Captain Lenhart of his youngest son's death. Miraculously Karl had appeared shortly afterward, to comfort his father, and Louise. The oldest Lenhart son had driven down the coast, from Portland, when he heard of the disaster that had hit Ocean Breeze. Even before Holly and Dr. Catrell had left the Lenhart mansion, Karl and Louise had named their new little son for his dead uncle. Captain Lenhart had seemed comforted by the gesture.

A tap on her door interrupted Holly's doleful musings. Seconds later, Gen Byrde stuck her head inside, and entered, bearing a steaming tray.

"This time, I fixed breakfast for you, too," she said. Holly noticed that her jade-colored eyes were red-rimmed from weeping. Les, she thought. As bad as his reputation had been in Ocean Breeze, there were those to mourn him. Margaret had wept uncontrollably, when she had regained consciousness. The girl had told a heartrending story about how Les had saved her life, by getting her up onto the jutting little shelf on the wall of the headland, when the first of the big swells hit.

The two of them had been roasting weiners on the little stretch of beach, and hadn't noticed the rising water in the darkness, until it was too late to get back to the yacht that Les had anchored near the mouth of the cove.

"Les hung onto the edge of the ledge with one hand, and held me on it with the other," Margaret had told them, between sobs. "I was numb all over, with the wet and cold. And I wanted to get down and go home to Daddy. But he wouldn't let me. He said there'd be more waves. They came, just like he said. All I could see was Les's head sticking out. Then, all at once, I couldn't see him anymore. But I felt his hand in the water, holding me, so I wouldn't wash away. When it receded, Les was gone. There wasn't room for us both on the ledge," Margaret had cried. "I guess I passed out, after that."

"She's been through a lot," Holly indicated the sleeping girl, keeping her voice lowered to a whisper. "I'll have my breakfast in the other room, so it won't disturb her."

"I wanted to talk to you," Gen said, when the two of them were alone in the small, cheery living room. "I wanted to tell you that I'm glad for you . . . and Key. I was bitter, at first, because he had brought you here. For some crazy reason, it doesn't seem to matter anymore, now that Les is gone. It was really Les all the time. I suppose you've heard rumors about him and me. I wanted Key to notice me, just to spite him." She glanced up at Holly, her ripe face looking almost peaceful for the first time since Holly had met her. "I feel free now," she said simply. "I think Les might have been right for me, if he could have settled down. A woman knows a thing like that. Only, he never seemed able to . . ."

Gen was right, Holly thought. A woman *did* know when a man was right for her. She had experienced that sense of knowing, for the first time, with Dr. Key Catrell.

There was only one thing wrong. Dr. Catrell thought that she was still engaged to Brian. He knew nothing of the scene in the hallway of the Lenhart mansion, or that she had refused to put Brian's ring back on her finger. And she *wanted* him to know, she thought.

There was only one way, and that was to *tell* him.

She flew into sudden action, rustling into her immaculate uniform, perching her crisp, black-banded cap on her dark head. Five minutes later, she stepped out into the morning sunlight, and hurried across the blacktop to Dr. Catrell's small office.

"It's all right, Holly," Dr. Catrell smiled at her. "Come on in. You might be interested in what Captain Lenhart has been discussing with me."

"I was just telling Dr. Catrell that I intend to turn the old mansion over to him," Captain said. "It's no place for Louise and Karl to bring up little . . . little Les." His aged voice cracked a little. "And I don't need it anymore to house my collection. My models washed away, last night, when the wave surged through town. It's just as well. It got to where I had no time for anything else."

"I don't understand," Holly said.

"We're going to turn the mansion

into that hospital this town has been needing," Dr. Catrell explained. "Captain has agreed to modernize it, if I'll run it."

"The Lesley Lenhart Memorial Hospital," Captain Lenhart said. "In memory of my son." His birdlike eyes lit on Holly's face. "I'm counting on you to stay and help Key run it," he said. "Be the . . . Super, isn't it?"

"I should have told you," Dr. Catrell said. "Miss Doran is spoken for elsewhere. The Dr. Merdahl who was here. I'm afraid our emergency prevented her from returning to San Francisco with him."

"But he can't come here and steal the best nurse Ocean Breeze has ever known," Captain Lenhart stated emphatically.

She was reminded of the speech she had made to Miss Lucas, at Sea Beach General, what seemed like an eon ago.

"That isn't quite what I meant, Captain," Dr. Catrell was saying. "Miss

Doran is engaged to Dr. Merdahl."

"No, Key," Holly heard herself saying. "Not anymore." She turned to Captain Lenhart. "I'd be proud to accept that job as Super," she told him, her own voice emphatic.

She was aware of Dr. Catrell's gray eyes on her, searching her face. "You sounded like a woman who knows what she wants," he remarked, when the dapper little man had gone. He arose from behind his desk, and came toward her.

"Yes, Key," she said, simply. "I am that kind of woman. For the first time in my life."

"I don't know what you think of headland G.P.'s," he said. "But if your opinion is favorable, I believe the housekeeper's cottage over at the new Lesley Lenhart Memorial Hospital could be fixed into a cozy dwelling. For two," he added, his gray eyes bright. Then, "I've decided to sell the motel to Gen. I think she has more right to it than I do."

"I'm glad," Holly said.

"Nobody's living in the cottage, now. And it's always unlocked," Dr. Catrell continued. He glanced at his watch. "If you're interested, I think there'll be just time to look it over, after we check on our hospital full of patients!"

"I'd like that, Doctor . . . Key." Holly's blue eyes sparkled with some new, inner glow.

"I hoped you would, darling."

She knew, with a sure, feminine knowledge, that he was going to kiss her. She yielded herself happily, thinking that it would take time to transform the Lenhart Mansion. And the cottage. Just as it would take time to rebuild the ravaged little town below the headland.

Now that Brian was no longer a part of her existence, she had time to spend here on this high headland, in Dr. Catrell's safe, gentle arms. A whole lifetime.

Other titles in the Linford Romance Library:

A YOUNG MAN'S FANCY
Nancy Bell

Six people get together for reasons of their own, and the result is one of misunderstanding, suspicion and mounting tension.

THE WISDOM OF LOVE
Janey Blair

Barbie meets Louis and receives flattering proposals, but her reawakened affection for Jonah develops into an overwhelming passion.

MIRAGE IN THE MOONLIGHT
Mandy Brown

En route to an island to be secretary to a multi-millionaire, Heather's stubborn loyalty to her former flatmate plunges her into a grim hazard.

WITH SOMEBODY ELSE
Theresa Charles

Rosamond sets off for Cornwall with Hugo to meet his family, blissfully unaware of the shocks in store for her.

A SUMMER FOR STRANGERS
Claire Hamilton

Because she had lost her job, her flat and she had no money, Tabitha agreed to pose as Adam's future wife although she believed the scheme to be deceitful and cruel.

VILLA OF SINGING WATER
Angela Petron

The disquieting incidents that occurred at the Vatican and the Colosseum did not trouble Jan at first, but then they became increasingly unpleasant and alarming.